Geoff Hart is a freelance novelist anc ,
interest in Bulgaria. His first book, *Bulgaria: Unfinished Business,* is an autobiographical travelogue telling the story of Geoff's and his wife's journey to Bulgaria with their dog and horses in a thirty year old horsebox. Moving forward and back in time the book gives an account of the joys and the hazards they meet on this journey, whilst simultaneously telling the often hilarious story of Geoff's ten year history with the country.

Geoff's first novel, *Second Time Lucky,* was published at the beginning of 2016 and is set twenty years into the future.

The Icon of Arbanasi

Geoff Hart

The Icon of Arbanasi

Geoff Hart

Published 2016

ISBN-13: 978-1534998209

I hold it true, whate'er befall;
   I feel it, when I sorrow most;
   'T is better to have loved and lost
Than never to have loved at all.

Alfred Lord Tennyson
From "In Memoriam"

Part One

Arbanasi
1686 AD

Chapter One

Rayna tried to recall the first time she had been aware of the advent of spring. She thought she must have been two or three, but had probably been older. Having at the time no understanding of the concept of re-birth and no knowledge of seasons, she thought that this was the beginning of life, not just hers, but all life. She had believed that she was there at the start. Consequently, when spring and then summer gave way to winter she assumed that this was the end; that the world and she with it would freeze over and cease to exist. When the days of winter turned to weeks and then months she concluded that this was some sort of purgatory that preceded the inevitable finality.

One day her sister, sensing her despair had said, "Don't worry, little Raya, soon it will be spring again."

This had been a moment of rejoicing and even now she could recall the relief that she had felt.

Now it was spring again, the favourite season for her and all rural people, and Rayna was in a mood to match the fine weather. As always at this time of year she was feeling good about the world, spiritually uplifted. The birds were singing in a tone that they only seem to use as springtime emerges, as if they were celebrating deliverance from the cold winter frosts. All the trees were turning green and the apple trees just outside her family's little house were already in blossom. The smell was heavenly and she could hear the bees doing their work amongst the pink flowers. Even the old oak tree which sat alongside the house was in leaf. It was a beautiful scene enhanced by the presence of Rayna herself. She had pulled her hair together into a bun and pushed it under her cap so now she could feel the warm sun on her bare neck. She knew that given how long it had been covered the skin on her neck would probably burn and that, even worse, freckles would appear. Nevertheless she could not resist the warm sensual feeling it gave her. Her sister, Boryana, said the spring sunshine made her feel lustful, especially when in the presence of the knife sharpening boy who visited the village every Saturday. Rayna smiled at her sister's shamelessness.

Rayna was just eighteen years old and her loveliness, evident since she was a young girl, was now flowering into womanhood. The young men of the village could hardly keep their eyes off her when she passed. Her thick black hair framed a perfectly proportioned face. Her smile could light up a room and her slender delicate body was as near to perfect as any one of these young men could ever imagine. However, so genuinely modest was she that she hardly noticed the attention. Often young women of such rare beauty are not liked by other girls and there were certainly some who claimed she was arrogant and held herself aloof from her contemporaries. Although there was little truth in this assertion, it did not stop it being said by those that were jealous of her good looks. In truth Rayna was an unassuming young woman and the majority of the villagers held her in the highest regard.

The village where Rayna lived with her family, Arbanasi, was high above the ancient city of Tarnovo. It was a delightful place with an aura of peace and serenity. The small dwellings smelt of burnt wood and spoke of modest lives. Trees surrounded the entire village, their broad, green leaves providing shade from the radiant sun. Dirt pathways wound throughout Arbanasi often coming to an end where one might least expect it. The summers were hot and the ground was fertile so like most of the people in the village Rayna's family grew all their own food in a small plot just outside the village. There was a strict division of labour within her family and most of the planting and tending of the vegetables fell to Rayna with occasional help from her elder sister, Boryana. Rayna enjoyed the work and last year there had been a particularly good harvest.

Despite this all Rayna's family had left to eat from the previous harvest were some old potatoes, already soft and wrinkly and extremely unappetising. It seemed as if they had eaten nothing other than potatoes for months now. They reminded Rayna of her grandfather's withered toes that poked out from his equally ancient sandals and when the poor girl conjured up this image she could not eat them at all. Her father said that, despite the good harvest, they always ran short of food because of the tithe that obliged them to give an unfair proportion of their crop to the lord.

"Why does one family need so much when the rest of us have so little to give?" she had asked him.

"Because Turks like to get fat on the labour of honest Bulgarian folk," was his reply.

Papa was always so cross, even in spring when the improving weather and the beauty of their surroundings ought to have made him happy as it did her. Rayna knew her father was a good man who loved his family above all else, but he had told her that he hated injustice and he could never live a happy life under the rule of a foreign power.

Rayna understood only a fraction of the things of which her father spoke. She had been born under Ottoman rule and this was simply the life she lived and Rayna loved life despite its uncertainties and its hardships. Sitting with her wise father with her sister and mother close by she was content and never considered that life could be otherwise. Why should she? Now it was spring she could look forward to some early crops and soon there would be cherries on the trees and strawberries on the bushes that she could pick as she passed. What bliss!

"Morning Raya, where have you hidden that beautiful black hair? Not under that old floppy cap, surely. Why do you wear that thing and deprive eager young men of the sight of your beautiful locks?"

Vladislav gave her a cheeky wink as he passed and she could feel the colour moving up her neck ready to cover her face with an unwelcome flush of embarrassment.

"I'll stick my hair where I like and it be none of your business, Vladislav Petrov, so keep your opinions to yourself."

And feeling that she had for once acquitted herself rather well she hurried on her way holding onto her cap to make sure that the aforementioned hair did not make an unwanted appearance. Everything would have been fine and she would have walked away having got the best of their brief encounter if only she had not looked round. There he stood staring at her with his hands on his slender hips and as she turned he gave her that wide knowing smile, his beautiful teeth made even whiter by the clear morning light.

"Damn him," she cursed to herself. "Damn that boy."

She could curse all she wanted because Vladislav himself and many of the older members of the village believed him to be blessed, watched over by the Virgin Mary herself. He was only nine years old when, wandering over the hills near his home tending his father's small herd of goats, he heard a mournful voice coming from the ground. The young Vladislav was terrified and rushed home to fetch his father.

"Papa, Papa, come quick! I have heard a voice coming from under the ground. The voice was crying and wailing. It must be a witch or a ghost. Come quick!"

Suddenly it dawned on the boy that he had left the goats unattended.

"Papa, quick I have forgotten about the goats, they will wander off. Maybe something terrible will happen to them."

His father tried to soothe his over-excited son although he was himself rather alarmed about what Vladislav was telling him as well as worrying about his goats.

"Vlado, calm down a little. Can you remember exactly where you left the goats, where you heard the sound?"

"Yes, it is the goat's favourite place on the mountain. Rich grass grows there. I will show you."

Petrov returned immediately with his son to the place where he had heard the voice. On the way there the father mulled over what young Vladimir had reported and by the time they arrived he believed he knew what his son had discovered. The sheep were still there apparently unconcerned by the mournful sounds, possibly even comforted by the expected presence of a human voice. Sure now about what he was seeking Petrov started digging while the young Vladislav listened intently as his father told him the legend of the icon of the Virgin Mary.

"Before Bulgaria fell under Ottoman rule, the St. Virgin Mary convent stood at the entrance to Arbanasi village. There is an old legend that says the nuns abandoned the convent shortly after the fall of the state to the Turkish soldiers. According to the legend they took the precious icon of the Virgin Mary and as they fled, covered the icon with cloths and hid it in the ground."

Vladislav was jumping around like a scalded cat while his father continued resolutely with his digging.

"Why did they hide it in the ground, Papa?" he asked.

"They hid it because it was holy and they were fearful should it fall into the hands of non-Christians," his father replied. "And I think they buried it because they had no time to find somewhere safe. The invaders were closing on them."

With Vladislav standing next to him with his mouth wide open and his eyes bulging, Petrov continued with his story.

"Many times since then people from our village have reported hearing a mournful cry coming across the hills but no one has ever been able to say exactly where the sound came from, until now."

Sure enough, just four feet underground Petrov found the icon wrapped in rags, but perfectly preserved. As he brushed the last covering of earth from the object the mournful voice stopped abruptly. The icon was inside a silver repousse cover, ornamented with patterns made by hammering on the reverse side. It was the silver repousse cover spoken of in the legend that told Petrov that it was indeed the precious icon of the Virgin Mary.

With great ceremony Petrov carefully handed the icon to his son who looked at it in awe.

"Maybe it is a sign from God," the father speculated. "You are the one who has rescued the icon from its burial place and brought it back into the world for all to see and wonder at. I think it will bring you much fortune, Vladislav."

The precious icon of the Virgin Mary, although regarded as special to Vladislav, now stood in the smallest most humble room within the village church where villagers, and others travelling through, often came to look on it.

*

Rayna hurried on still feeling foolish over her encounter with Vladislav until she reached the family's field. The land was flat with rich fertile soil. It was not a large field, but it was sufficient. The land was bordered on three sides by a hedge, but was otherwise open to the path that led back into the village. Rayna's family had been tilling this soil for generations and she was glad to be the latest in a long line. It gave her a sense of place.

She tucked her long skirt up to allow a little sun onto her winter white legs, put her basket down by the hedge to shield her meagre lunch from the sun's rays and immediately set to work. Rayna had the sunniest of dispositions and very soon her good humour returned. An hour later she was working away and singing softly to herself when her older sister arrived to join her in the field.

"You seem very full of yourself, Raya. Been flirting with that Petrov boy again, I wouldn't wonder."

"Flirting with him, why would I flirt with him? I hate him."

"Aye, I can see that by the way you look at him; real hateful, it is."

And so the day passed with her sister, Boryana teasing her in that gentle way of hers from which it was impossible to take offence.

That evening, Rayna was sitting outside on the yard with her father while Boryana and her mother busied themselves within the small house in the preparation of the evening meal. She loved her father's company especially when it was just him and her.

"Papa, why do you always call us Bulgarians? I mean we live in Arbanasi village, in the region of Tarnovo. We are surely Christians, not Bulgarians – whatever that means."

"We are Christians certainly, though the Sultan would have it otherwise, but we are also Bulgarians. This is our land and our country, Raya, even though the Turks refuse us the name. This is Bulgaria, girl and you are Bulgarian. Never forget that."

Quietly Rayna made a promise to herself that she would try and remember what her father had told her. She did not fully understand what he was saying, but something in his tone and demeanour indicated to her that what he had said was important. She would remember that she was a Bulgarian, if she remembered nothing else.

The following day was washing day and Rayna along with her sister was busy helping her mother at the small stream that ran down the hill and eventually flowed into the mighty River Yantra. Crouching by the stream she could see right across the grassy plain on the opposite bank that ran on almost as far as the eye could see eventually giving way to the forest. For hundreds of years this had been common land, used by everyone in the village who had stock to graze. Now the land was owned by the local feudal lord, granted to him by the Sultan's agent in return for providing local men as soldiers to fight alongside Turks in the Polish–Ottoman War. Sixteen young men from Arbanasi and the smaller villages around had been sent to fight and not a single one returned, but as if that was not punishment enough the village had also lost claim to the huge parcel of excellent pasture land. Those villagers with herds exceeding ten head of sheep or six head of cattle were still allowed to graze their animals on the common on payment of a further land tax known as an ispenc. In the near distance Rayna could see Vladislav with his small flock of sheep. She knew that he refused to pay the ispenc and worried about what could happen to him if this fact was discovered. The boy was so reckless.

"Someday something terrible will happen to him," she thought to herself. "And even the icon will not be able to protect him then."

*

At home in Anatolia Bayram was much admired by the eligible young women for his thick black hair. He was not vain and so his hair was rarely brushed falling onto his shoulders in casual untended curls. His eyebrows were thin and narrow below which his eyes shone brightly with the vigour of youth. He had an unremarkable nose and his angular cheekbones ran down towards a determined jaw. Despite his youth he already had a manly physique. When he walked he glided with an athletic grace giving the impression that running would be easier than walking. Bayram was handsome in an understated way,

Despite being admired by his peers Bayram was glad of the chance to leave Anatolia, not because he was unhappy there, but simply because he yearned to travel. Twelve months earlier his father had been appointed as the Sanjakbey, the military leader and Governor of the Tarnovo region, far away from Istanbul, the seat of power of the Empire. Three weeks ago Bayram and his mother had joined him here. His father was at least outwardly pleased with his appointment. As one of the Sultan's regular servicemen, one of the so- called spahi, he might have expected to be offered land close to home with all the rights that land ownership conferred. Instead he had been posted to the Tarnovo district and although this posting gave him more land and a higher level of authority it took him away from the political mainstream. Bayram's mother quite clearly thought the posting degrading and hated finding herself among agricultural peasants far from the bazaars and the fashions of the capital city. Her husband pointed out to her that he was one of few Sanjakbeys accountable directly to the Sultan proving that he still had the ear of the supreme ruler, but she scoffed at this.

"We have been banished from civilisation to live among peasants and barbarians." she exclaimed.

Her husband more than anything wanted a quiet life and the posting suited him quite well. He was confident that his wife would soon settle and his son, Bayram, already seemed happy enough.

It was certainly true that Bayram was happy. Although Tarnovo lacked the splendour of Turkish cities it had a charm that was hard to define. The people lived simple lives that seemed sufficient for their modest needs. Certainly they appeared content with what their God provided for them. How often had he seen them in the street in small clusters, just chatting and laughing?

One thing that had especially caught Bayram's eye was the beauty of the young women in his new home with their angular faces and wonderfully slim bodies. One in particular was stunning. That morning he had passed her working in a field with an older friend or sister near the village of Arbanasi. The girl was so ravishing and had such magnetic beauty that once his eyes had fallen upon her it became an extreme act of will to draw his glance away and for quite some time he lacked both the will and inclination to do so. Consequently he stared at her for some time. The other girl had spoken her name, but the local tongue was so unfamiliar to him he had not caught it properly. Later that day he intended to pass that way again for a second look.

Unbeknown to Bayram the girl in the field had noticed him too. Given the way in which he had locked his eyes on her she could hardly fail to. So when he returned later in the day she was already looking out for him. This time he was on horseback, riding a beautiful chestnut Arab. With its finely chiselled head, long arching neck and high tail carriage, the purebred horse was striking. Its entire appearance exuded energy, intelligence, courage and nobility. To Rayna's eyes the horse was slim and handsome, just like the young man riding him.

"Dobŭr den." Bayram called. "Good day" was about the limit of his Bulgarian.

"Ignore him!" Boryana commanded. "He is a filthy Turk and what's more he is the son of the Sanjakbey."

Needless to say, despite her apparent antipathy to him, Boryana had also noticed the dark handsome young man and had made it her business to find out who he was.

"What is a Sanjakbey?" Rayna enquired of her sister.

"He is the bastard to whom we pay taxes and the man who steals our crops so we go hungry. That young man looks so sleek and healthy because he lives off our crops without lifting a finger in their growing. Papa says the Turks are our enemies and you will do well to remember that. Come on, these tomatoes won't plant themselves."

Reluctantly Rayna did as her sister had instructed her, returning to her work, but she could see that the smile on the young man's lips was intended only for her.

Bayram was an only child and had left all of his friends behind in Istanbul. Had this not been the case he would have been telling his friend, Ayaz all about the girl in the field. So smitten was he that he just could not keep his news to himself.

"Mother, I have seen this young girl in the village. She is so beautiful that I can't stop looking at her and I think she has noticed me too. I so want to speak to her, but I do not understand their native tongue."

"What! Are you mad? First your father drags us to this land of barbarians and then you start drooling over some native girl, some local trollop. Have you left your brains in Anatolia? Of course the stupid little bitch has noticed you. Do you think there is a young woman anywhere in this district who has not noticed you? If you see her again spit at her and if I see her I will have her arrested for prostitution."

Bayram started to protest, being particularly offended by the suggestion that the innocent looking young girl was no more than a whore, but his mother silenced him.

"I will hear no more about it, is that clear?"

Bayram knew better than to argue. How stupid he had been to even mention the girl. His mother thought everyone outside Istanbul was a peasant and he should have foreseen her reaction. He was boiling with indignation on behalf of the girl and at his own folly.

Two nights later, Rayna was on her way home from the vegetable garden where she had been working. It was one of those spring evenings where the sun seems reluctant to set, its once brilliant rays shining less brightly than earlier in the day, but still with a touch of warmth. Rounding a bend in the path Rayna saw Vladislav coming towards her driving his small flock of sheep from the field where they had been grazing back to his father's house. He was a decent and good looking young man and they had known each other since they were children.

Both families assumed that one day they would marry, as did most of the village. Indeed, despite their play acting Rayna and Vladislav probably assumed this too. Rayna was certainly fond of him, but in the last few days her emotions had been thrown into turmoil by her encounter with the young foreign stranger. She had been thinking of him constantly and she was experiencing feelings she had never known before. The whole thing was disturbing yet somehow exciting. Almost overnight her feelings for Vladislav had changed also, becoming less intense and more filial in their nature. She still worried about him though and when she saw him coming along the path with his flock she approached him immediately to tell him of her concerns about him using the large pasture by the river without paying the ispenc.

"Raya, you worry so. I will not be noticed amongst all the other old shepherds and farmers, and what's more we cannot afford to pay it. Why should we anyway? It has been common land for centuries. Why should we suddenly pay some foreign lord for the privilege of exercising our birth right?"

Although recognising it to be futile, Rayna persisted with her argument. "That is just it. Because you are a young man and all the others are old crocks you do stand out. If you are caught the soldiers will not be interested in your birth right. They will simply apply the law."

"And whose law is that? It is certainly not one I recognise," he replied.

"Like it or not, it is the law we live under and you must respect it," said Rayna.

Her frustration and anger was now showing in her face, but Vladislav did not seem to notice, or if he did he made no attempt at appeasement.

"They can all rot in hell including that silky faced little bastard who has been making eyes at you!"

Rayna looked at him both astonished and embarrassed. Denial seemed the only option, anyway she had never even spoken to him.

"I don't know what you are talking about!"

"If only that were true, Rayna," he replied and with that he waved his stick at his small herd and drove them on towards home.

Rayna was physically and emotionally shaken up. "What is the matter with me?" she asked herself aloud.

She liked to think of herself as a rational young woman and on one level she could see that the whole thing was ridiculous, but emotionally she just could not help herself. At the very least she was fascinated by the boy, but something told her it was more than that. She was drawn to him in a way she could not explain. She could not stop thinking about him and there and then she resolved not to fight it. She would not obey her sister's warning or take heed of what her father would think. Much as it pained her she could not put Vladislav's feelings ahead of hers. She would seek the young man out and try and speak with him and see where that took her. Bayram too was unable to shake the thought of Rayna from his mind and a few hours later, as Rayna lay in her bed struggling for sleep, he stood outside her family's humble home partially concealed by the great oak tree and dreamed of holding her.

Whether it was because his mind was not on the job or simply because his flock was in a truculent mood it was hard to say, but the fact is it took Vladislav an hour longer than usual to get his sheep home that evening. After his conversation with Rayna his mind was in a whirl. She had approached him with the best of intentions, clearly worried for his safety and he had treated her badly in return. He believed passionately in his right to graze his flock by the river without hindrance and without paying taxes to some foreign power. However, in his heart he knew that to simply carry on without regard to the dangers was foolhardy. Rayna had done no more than point out what he already knew. Also it demonstrated, not for the first time, that she cared about him which surely ought to please him. Then he had thrown that at her about the scrawny Turk who he had seen mooning over her. What was she supposed to make of that? He was hardly the first boy to notice her. Her beauty captivated every young man in the village. Then why did she go red in the face when he mentioned the Turk? He shook his head as if trying to rid himself of these stupid jealous thoughts.

"For God's sake, get a grip of yourself, Vladislav Petrov," he said to himself sternly. Perhaps the sheep were listening, but Vladislav Petrov certainly wasn't.

*

Rayna's father, Vasil, sat on the bench with a group of his friends. The bench was situated in the village square, shaded from the afternoon sun by the old church. They had been enjoying a glass of rakia together talking and laughing about the old days of their youth, but as the alcohol started to take hold their thoughts and conversation turned to current concerns and immediately the youth of the day came under attack.

"One thing is for sure," said Boyan, "There is no way we would have put up with these new taxes. What is the matter with the young men? Have they no backbone?"

His friend Nikolay was not so sure. "You are not being fair, Boyan. We put up with what these Turks did to us in our day. The reason was the same then as it is now. Any attempt at rebellion is met with death and slaughter. They are absolute tyrants. They even take the strongest young Bulgarian boys from their mothers and turn their minds so even they are against us. Without help from outside there is nothing we can do. It is hopeless."

"Petrov's youngster, Vlado, tells me there is talk of another uprising," Vasil reported. "Rostislav Stratimirovic is involved and is said to have the support of Russia. According to young Petrov there are a lot of young men from Arbanasi ready to take up arms as soon as the word is given. He believes it may all start right here."

His friends were now paying close attention and they gathered more closely together like a gaggle of elderly conspirators.

"Well I'm in!" asserted Boyan as the adrenalin started pumping through his old veins.

13

"Don't be ridiculous, Boyan," Vasil protested. "They don't want old fools like us getting in the way. Fighting is a young man's game."

"Maybe, but what do young men know about strategy?" Boyan retorted. "Who is to command them?"

"There speaks a man who doesn't even have a strategy to get the better of his wife!" said Nikolay, rather unkindly and the whole group fell about laughing at Boyan's expense.

"Well if any of you think you can control her you are welcome to her. I would rather fight the Turkish army single handed!"

Boyan's friends laughed at this too and equilibrium was restored. As more rakia was imbibed the subject of rebellion gave way to more homely matters, but as the group split up, most wandered home with Vasil's news at the forefront of their minds. Most of them had sons themselves and no father wanted to see his son butchered by the Ottoman troops or even worse by the janissary corps.

A particularly cruel form of oppression exercised by the Turks was the blood tax (the devsirme), which had been levied since the fifteenth century. Bulgarian families were forced to give up their best male children who were then 'purified' and educated in exceptional Muslim fanaticism. They made up the janissary corps and became the mainstay of the Ottoman authorities, often used to enforce Ottoman law against their Bulgarian kinsmen. Neither Vasil nor his friends would be ashamed to say they were terrified of them.

Recently Russia, Saxony, Brandenburg and Bavaria had joined the Holy League against the Ottoman Turkish Empire. Rostislav Stratimirovic, a descendant of the medieval Shishman dynasty, was determined that Bulgaria would get some benefit from this new alliance and did his best to exploit the international situation in Bulgaria's favour. In an attempt to establish friendly relations with the Russian Patriarch Joachim he was now in Moscow trying to build support in preparation for the uprising that he planned to ignite in the capital city, Tarnovo and in the surrounding area.

Meanwhile, in Arbanasi, unbeknown to his father, Boyan's son, Todor had adopted the role that his father had said no youngster could perform adequately, i.e. that of local leader. He had been told by Stratimirovic to organise the young men of Arbanasi and the nearby villages in readiness for the fight. Mature beyond his years Todor was a natural leader; a young man that without effort could command the respect of his peers. Todor had from his father a strong sense of justice and he had grown up nurturing the idea that one day Bulgarians would free themselves from Ottoman oppression. He was aware that the Turks had recently been defeated by Austrian forces and the long held belief that the Ottoman Empire was invincible was diminishing across Europe. Todor believed with a passion that Bulgaria's moment was at hand.

*

Having made the decision to try and speak to the young man on the Arab steed, Rayna was encountering practical problems in the execution of her plan. The most obvious difficulty was the lack of a shared language, although she believed that somehow this could be overcome. She was more vexed by the question of how they could actually meet. She could hardly march into the Turkish quarter in Tarnovo and call on him. Also if his father was indeed the local lord their home would be like a fortress. This much she had worked out for herself, but in her naivety she had not yet properly considered that the whole idea of relations between the son of the Sanjakbey and a young peasant girl was unthinkable. Given her friendly disposition and helpful nature, not to mention her beauty, any mother in Arbanasi would be happy to have her as their daughter in law and the idea that others would regard her as an unsuitable match for their son had not truly crossed her mind. She was aware of her own father's antipathy towards the Turks, but did not understand the basis of this. In truth Rayna lived within the moment and had little knowledge of the oppression and resentment that existed within her world. Her father had told her never to forget she was a Bulgarian and she was determined both to take pride in this fact and in turn make her father proud of her on account of this. She did not realise that for her father, and indeed for most of the population, hating Turks was an integral part of being a Bulgarian. If there was a moral question for her it was simply this: she was by assumption practically promised to Vladislav and yet she found herself fascinated by someone else.

With the whole matter unresolved Rayna went about her work. For the first time in her life she realised she was happiest when alone. She loved and looked up to her elder sister, Boryana, and usually was never happier than in her company, but now she found that she wanted to be alone with her thoughts, free to indulge in the wildest of fantasies without the interruption of having to be civil to someone. Uncharacteristically she found herself engineering situations so that she could be on her own. On this particular occasion she had told her sister that she had almost finished the planting and that Boryana should do the chores at home to give their mother a break. Boryana was not used to her little sister being so assertive, but if she did find it odd this was more than overcome by the fact that she hated planting. Furthermore it was Saturday and the boy who sharpened knives would be calling today. Boryana would have to make sure that her mother had a good number of blunt knives so as to delay him as long as possible. For Rayna her little white lie meant she could be alone, but it also meant that she had a lot of planting to do and it would be some time before she could return home. She had already been afield for four hours and was feeling tired, but she could see that she had at least another three hours of work to complete.

"Rayna, I came to say I was sorry. I spoke far too sharply to you the other day when your only crime was to worry about me."

Rayna had been deep in thought about the young Turk and these thoughts were causing physical reactions within her which were both pleasant and slightly shameful to her. So the sudden sound of Vladislav's familiar voice both startled and embarrassed her.

"Rayna, are you alright?" Vladislav's concerns only made things worse, but slowly she recovered herself.

"Yes, I'm alright. It is just the heat and I have been working for hours without a break."

"Well take a break now, Rayna, so we can talk," Vladislav replied, but Rayna was not at all keen to have the type of conversation that Vladislav intended.

"I can't talk now I promised Mama and Boryana that I would finish this planting today and you can see how much there is to do."

"Well, I'll just have to help you then and we can talk after."

Rayna was torn. She desperately needed some help with the planting otherwise she would be there until sundown. However, she was equally clear that she wanted to avoid any sort of heart to heart with Vladislav. In the end she just left the decision to be made for her. Vladislav took a plant from Rayna's tray and set to work in the dark and fertile soil. He worked almost in silence and Rayna realised that he was saving the intended conversation until the planting was finished and he could have her full attention.

After about two hours the work was all but complete and Rayna was getting increasingly anxious about what Vladislav would have to say.

"Ah, I wondered why you were taking so long!"

Rayna and Vladislav looked up to see Rayna's sister, Boryana approaching.

"There's me worrying about you and here you are flirting with Vladislav Petrov again. Try and keep your eyes off him, Raya. He has his own work to do, don't you Vlado, or are you the one to blame? Yes, maybe you are? After all I have found you in our field, so you must have come looking for Rayna. You are the scoundrel after all."

Boryana laughed at her own teasing, Vladislav looked embarrassed and Rayna just looked relieved.

"I just needed to talk to your sister about something."

For once Vladislav found himself stumbling over his words. Boryana, ignoring the young man's earnestness and discomfort, continued to tease him.

"That is fine, go ahead. Rayna and I are listening, aren't we, Raya?"

"I needed to talk to your sister in private," Vladislav protested.

"I believe you that you wanted to be private, but in order to talk? How stupid do you think I am, Master Petrov?"

Rayna took the opportunity that her sister's good humour had provided for her.

"Come on, Boryana, leave the poor boy in peace. We are finished here now. Let's get ourselves home before Mama sends out a search party."

Vladislav went to object, but the words died on his lips. He knew he was no match for Rayna's spirited sister.

When Vladislav arrived home, his thoughts about Rayna were soon put aside. His close friend Todor was waiting for him on the street, just outside his parents' house. He looked both anxious and angry. Vladislav had never seen Todor so worked up and it unsettled him. Unlike Vladislav, Todor had lost all traces of boyhood. His forehead was large and imposing above bushy eyebrows which were impossibly straight. His eyes were a rich mahogany colour. Todor's most striking feature was his thick black beard. It highlighted the frown that was now placed upon his mouth and his square jaw somehow made him seem even more authoritative than his aura already suggested. He was strongly built with cords of muscle knotting his neck and shoulders.

Todor started berating Vladislav as soon as he saw him approaching.

"You and your big mouth! What the hell are you doing talking to Rayna's father about the planned uprising? You could get us all killed. You might yet!"

Vladislav looked crestfallen. Although he could see at once that he had been wrong to talk to Vasil Kolev he instinctively tried to defend his actions.

"Vasil Kolev is a true Bulgarian. He would never let us down," he asserted.

"No of course not," said Todor sarcastically. "Which is why he got drunk on rakia and repeated your story to every ne'er-do-well in the village, including my father!"

Vlado went bright red and gave up any pretence that his actions had been justified.

"Oh, my God! What should we do now, Todor?"

"We, we? *We* should do nothing. You should keep your mouth shut and I will try and sort this out before we all end up hanging from a tree."

Vladislav opened his mouth to speak, but Todor raised his hand for silence. Slowly his mood changed from anger to disappointment which hurt Vladislav more grievously.

"If there was anyone I was sure I could count on it was you, Vlado, my best friend and yet look what you have done."

With that Todor turned solemnly on his heel and walked away. His own words felt bitter on his lips as he left Vladislav to lick his wounds alone.

*

Another week had passed and Rayna had started to give up hope that she would see the handsome Turkish boy again. During this time she had also managed to avoid Vladislav to the point where it was beginning to be obvious that she was shunning his company. Besides anything else it just wasn't fair to him. He had done nothing to deserve such poor treatment and she could see that he was slightly bewildered.

She was walking alone on the lane on her way to the family field to check the crops she had planted, having virtually decided to put the matter of the young stranger behind her. Just on the point of making this decision she heard the sound of hooves cantering along the path. She knew instantly that it was a Turkish rider, because from the sound she could tell that the horse was shod and no local horses had shoes. Her heart was in her mouth in anticipation that it could be the young son of the local lord. Suddenly the horse and rider came shooting into view almost knocking her to the ground as they rounded the bend. Although the young rider showed great skill in bringing the horse to a stop almost from a full gallop, Rayna was terrified as the steed loomed over her. She yelled at him in her native tongue that Bayram could not understand, but the tone of her words were clear enough. Rayna fought her way out from the bush in which she had sought refuge and got quickly to her feet in an attempt to regain her dignity. Bayram stared at her with his mouth open. He was sure he had never in his entire life seen anything so beautiful as this girl. Her cheeks, flushed red with anger and exertion, completed the heavenly vision.

"You stupid man, you and your nag could have killed me! This is a well-used footpath. What if I had been an old woman? What then?"

Bayram got off his horse and offered his hand to help her to her feet although it was quite clear that she had managed unaided. She pulled both hands away in a defiant gesture, not yet ready to forgive him. One of his father's servants had been teaching Bayram some native phrases and he decided it was a good time to try them out.

"Zdraveĭ! Kazvam se Bayram."

"Do you think I care what your stupid name is?" she replied. "An apology might be a start."

"Bayram," he repeated pointing to himself. "You?"

With this Bayram pointed his finger at Rayna. Despite herself she found his ponderous attempts to communicate with her both amusing and endearing. His naivety was such he seemed completely oblivious to her displeasure. Suddenly her anger left her as quickly as it had flared up.

"Rayna." she smiled. "My name is Rayna."

Chapter Two

Bayram had never felt like this before. All of a sudden the light of the sun seemed brighter, the mountains more magnificent and the flowers more colourful than he had ever seen them. His heart was uplifted and his eyes saw nothing but beauty. He was again riding his chestnut Arab and together they seemed to be floating on air. A short while spent with the girl had set his heart free. He longed to touch her and hold her tightly to him. Bayram guessed that he must be in love. Surely, nothing but love could feel this good.

Rayna was sure that she had never seen such a handsome man. She believed she would be able to look at the young stranger's face for ever, the bone structure was so fine and perfectly symmetrical. Somehow too his inner tenderness showed on his face; his eyes were soft and there was a gentleness in his smile. Nor had she ever seen such a fine horse. She laughed to herself that in her shock and anger she had referred to the glistening Arab gelding as a nag, not that the boy had understood the insult nor much else that she said. With a broad grin she recalled how he had tried so hard to talk to her in her native tongue and how everything had come out wrong. She had laughed at him, but he had only smiled back and continued to try. For modesty's sake she had tried not to be so forthcoming, but with him standing there before her she just could not stop smiling. Somehow he made her heart glad.

Rayna did much of her thinking as she walked home at night and this particular evening she had more to think about than ever before. The sun was just setting giving the darkening sky a magnificent red tinge. Towards the east, away from the setting sun the first stars were appearing. Rayna was completely bowled over by the young Turk with the sparkling eyes and even a girl of her limited experience could see that he was very taken with her. However, as unworldly as she was, Rayna had learned enough to know that their feelings for each other would face obstacles. Her sister's words came into her head. "Papa says the Turks are our enemies and you will do well to remember that." She did remember and she also recalled her pledge to her father not to forget that she was Bulgarian. But did being Bulgarian automatically imply a hatred for Turks? This did not seem right to her, after all she knew of many Bulgarians who were not good people, so in the same way it could not be so that all Turks were bad. She had looked into the eyes of the young man who called himself Bayram. She would not believe that he was a bad person.

As she often did, her sister was coming along the path to meet her. Boryana gave a cheerful wave as her younger sister came into view. All their lives the two girls had been as close as any two sisters could be. They shared everything including their innermost thoughts and usually Rayna would have been breathlessly describing her meeting with Bayram, telling Boryana how wonderful he was. On this occasion, however, she hesitated. If her sister regarded her feelings towards Bayram as a problem she would be devastated. It was not a problem. It was something wonderful and she would not be able to bear it if her sister, the person she loved most in all the world were to cast a shadow over the whole affair. In the end though she could not help herself and her feelings spilled out.

Boryana listened silently to her little sister, unable to understand how these feelings could have arisen so suddenly between Rayna and the young Turkish boy right under her nose. She was worried. Rayna could see that in her face, but the younger girl had underestimated her sister and her sisters love for her. Boryana, a pretty girl herself, knew that Rayna had exceptional beauty. She also knew that she had a warm and open heart and she had always believed that one day she would give her heart completely. Unlike her parents, she had not believed that Vladislav would be the one, but it had never occurred to her that Rayna would fall in love with a Turk. Great tribulation and conflict lay ahead, she knew this. Her father would be livid when he heard and so would the boy's father, even more so. Both parents would forbid it. She looked at her sister whose open face was concentrating on hers waiting for a reaction. Slowly a gentle smile spread across Boryana's face. She took her young sister in her arms and held her tight.

"Don't worry, Raya. Somehow we will work it out."

If anyone was going to break her sister's heart that person would not be her.

All evening while Rayna sat mooning over Bayram Boryana was deep in her own thoughts. She was desperately thinking about what she could do to advance her sister's cause. She realised that she must somehow push the matter along before it was put to her father so that it was harder for him to put a stop to it. The more she thought about it the clearer it became that the boy would have to be the one to take the initiative. Rayna may be an exceptional beauty, but she was a poor peasant girl. Bayram, if that was his name, was from the most powerful family in the region. It was up to him to stand tall and she intended to seek him out and make sure he realised it.

The two sisters had shared a mattress in the small two room house since childhood. Their mattress was stuffed with straw and lay on ropes strung across a wooden frame. Other than the bed there was some very basic furniture, a bench, two stools, a table and a wooden chest where they kept their winter clothes and a few precious possessions. The floor was hard earth. Despite the simplicity of the room it was to the sisters a cosy haven where at night they could share their thoughts and secrets.

That night neither of them were finding sleep easy. Given they were both wide awake Boryana decided to outline her plan to Rayna. When Boryana said that she intended to speak to Bayram, Rayna was not too sure what she thought about the idea. However, she had sought guidance from her elder sister throughout her life and had almost always followed her advice. Now was not the time to do otherwise.

"What are you going to say to him?" she asked anxiously.

Boryana was not entirely sure what she intended to say, but did not want her sister to know that.

"I will ask him what his intentions are," she replied, aware that this was not much of an answer.

Rayna looked at her quizzically, fearing for the first time that her sister's plan may not be as well thought through as she had hoped. However, she said nothing.

"So tomorrow, Raya, I will go to the field and you can stay at home and help Mama. He is bound to come to the field looking for you so I will get my opportunity to speak to him then."

Rayna was also certain that Bayram would ride out to the field to see her and she had been desperately looking forward to it. More than that she worried about how disappointed he would be when she was not there. Her sister read her thoughts.

"Don't worry, Raya. There will be plenty of opportunities to see him after that."

"I know," replied Rayna, "But he will be so disappointed that it is you there when he was expecting me."

Realising what she had said Rayna looked embarrassed. Her sister smiled at her.

"I know I am not as pretty as you, little sister, but young men are not usually disappointed to see me!"

"I didn't mean that. I just…"

The two girls burst into laughter and after a goodnight hug, turned over to sleep.

*

Bayram had been awake half the night and had risen with the sun. He wondered at what time Rayna would get to the field. Given the heat later in the day he was certain it would be quite early. At eight, after a quickly consumed breakfast, he could not wait any longer. He told the stable boy to saddle his horse and soon he was on the path that led to the field where Rayna could usually be found. Seeing a young girl at work there he quickened his pace, but as he drew near he realised it was the girl he had seen working with Rayna on that day when he had noticed her for the first time.

She lifted her head as he approached and now he could see that this girl was unmistakably Rayna's sister. Although the sisters were facially alike, this girl was sturdier with broader shoulders and hips. Her hour glass figure was very near perfect, but she lacked the delicacy and allure of her younger sister. To his surprise she spoke to him in his own language wishing him a good morning.

"Good morning," he replied. "I am Bayram."

"I know who you are. I have come here to speak to you."

Boryana spoke with confidence and poise. She looked the young man up and down. It was not hard to understand why her sister had fallen for him. He was one of the most attractive men she had seen for a long time. Politely Bayram dismounted from his horse not wanting to hold a conversation with the girl from above.

"How is it that you can speak my language?" he asked her, "and so well."

"I was in service to the Sanjakbey who preceded your father," she informed him. "I hated it so when he left I did too. My father was never happy about it anyway."

"I have heard the previous Sanjakbey was not a very nice man. You would have found my father very different," said Bayram.

"I decided not to take that chance," she said simply.

Bayram could see that this girl knew her own mind and would not be charmed by him or anyone else. He hoped very much that she had come to speak to him in support of her sister's feelings for him, not to speak against it. She would make an exceptional ally, but a formidable opponent.

"I wanted to speak to you, because my younger sister, Rayna, has strong feelings for you and believes that you feel the same about her. Is that so?"

Bayram was still unclear where this was going.

"I can think of nothing but her." he said honestly.

"Well, that is at least a start," she replied. "I will not allow her to be hurt."

Bayram could see clearly that this girl only had her sister's interests at heart.

"What is your name?" he asked.

"Boryana," she replied.

"Boryana, I would never hurt her. I have not been in love before, so I cannot be sure, but I think I love your sister. I know it sounds crazy. I have only just met her, but she makes me feel so incredibly nice inside. I cannot explain the feeling because I do not understand it myself. She makes everything in the world seem different."

He stopped, not knowing how to continue. Boryana smiled at him. He could see that she was a very beautiful girl too. He could look at her objectively because unlike that of her sister, her smile did not turn him to jelly.

*

Yelling at his friend had momentarily made Todor feel better, but now, a few days later he regretted it. His anger at Vladislav had been justified, but having told his friend he no longer trusted him he now felt alone and isolated. He had taken on a heavy commission from Rostislav Stratimirovic, the man leading the planned rebellion. He was proud to serve, but he was starting to feel the pressure. He was terrified of making a mistake that would undo everything and now he had lost his confidant, Vladislav. Briefly, Todor considered talking to his father, maybe even asking for his advice, but he quickly dismissed the notion. He knew that if he spoke to him his father would want to get involved too and this would just give Todor something else to worry about.

Todor instinctively felt that he and his friends were in danger. He knew why Vladislav had chosen to speak to Vasil Kolev. His friend would not be able to admit to it, but it was tied into his feelings about Rayna. He wanted to show her father that he was a brave and honourable Bulgarian, and would make a fitting husband for Kolev's daughter. It was true, as Vladislav had said, that Kolev himself was an honourable man as were his group of elderly friends, but old men talk and talk was dangerous. Todor would have liked to speak to Rostislav Stratimirovic and let him decide what to do, but he was out of the country trying to seek help from potential allies who themselves were suffering at the hands of the Turks. In the end he concluded that he would have to get his inner group together and decide on what to do. Somehow he needed to find out whether the information about their plans had leaked beyond Kolev and his friends. This inner group would of course include Vladislav and unfortunately he would have to humiliate his friend by telling the others what Vladislav had done.

The group of young men had made a point of coming together in a different location each time and the next meeting was due to be held at the village grain store. Todor had put the word out that the meeting would be brought forward to that afternoon. When Vladislav heard that they were to assemble at the grain store later that day he was unsure whether Todor would want him to come. However, his friend Angel gave him some sensible advice.

"Vladislav, if he did not want you at the meeting you would not know about it. It is as simple as that."

Angel was of course correct. Vladislav would be there to face up to what he had done.

Like his comrades Angel could see that it was going to be virtually impossible to avoid bloodshed. This was not on account of Vladislav's folly, but something that had always been inevitable once the decision had been reached that oppression by a foreign power was simply not to be tolerated. Angel believed in the cause and knew what he must do and when the fight came he would do his duty, hard as it would fall to him. However, he had been brought up to detest violence and taking the life of another person was abhorrent to Angel. His parents were devout Christians in the old fashioned sense and he had been taught love and forgiveness from the cradle. But even these finest of Christian values could not easily be applied in dealing with cruel and pitiless oppressors. For Angel the greatest gift God had bestowed on man was free will and the right to exercise it freely. Even for a Christian there came a time to fight.

Also weighing on Angel was the secrecy that he was required to maintain even with regard to his parents. He had never held a secret from his mother and father, but talking to them was impossible. He knew this. He knew it was unthinkable not only because they would try to stop him, but also because he had given his friends his word. They had all made an oath of silence and he feared that his good friend Vladislav would pay dearly for breaking it.

The twelve young men who formed the inner circle of Todor's potential forces gathered solemnly in the grain store early that afternoon. One by one they seated themselves on the raised timber platforms used for drying the grain. The building had a pungent smell, a combination of smoke from the fires that were lit under the elevated platforms to dry the produce and deter insects and a fermented smell that grain can acquire after long storage. The rebel forces were brave to a man, but it was impossible not to feel some trepidation if, as they all suspected, the moment was at hand. Todor addressed the meeting while his friend Vladislav waited for the wrath of his comrades to envelop him.

*

Bayram was back on his horse, but this time he was in no hurry and, given the heat, his young Arab was glad of the opportunity to walk home at a leisurely pace. Bayram needed time to think. Boryana had been quite clear with him. Her father would be horrified at the idea of a match between his daughter and a Turk and she anticipated that his father would find the idea absurd and forbid it completely. She was right of course. He could see that now. He had not told her that he had already spoken to his mother about Rayna and he certainly did not want her to know about his mother's dreadful reaction. He was ashamed of it. The girl had also told him clearly that it was up to him to make it work. Rayna was a simple girl, subject completely to the authority of her family. He, on the other hand, was the son of the Sanjakbey and, Boryana insisted, must have some power in his own right. Bayram had foolishly agreed with this assumption, not wanting the girl to think him weak. This was just stupid pride. He was not sure if he did have any power to get his own way. Up until now the need to assert himself had never properly arisen. But now it had arisen and he must work out how to approach the matter.

He suspected that if he again spoke to his mother she would not even give him a hearing, also she may really lose her temper and do something rash. She had been in a bad humour since their arrival in Tarnovo province and was best left alone until she was more settled. His mother was an emotional woman and one could just never be sure of her. His father on the other hand was a much more measured person.

However, he would be shocked and his first response would be to tell Bayram that the whole thing was impossible. His parents had for all he knew already selected a Sunni girl from a wealthy family to be his bride. The more he thought about it the more hopeless it seemed. There was an immense difference in wealth, power and religion and the problem was beginning to overwhelm him.

*

"What do you think of the new Sanjakbey, Bilal?" asked Ekrem. "He seems a bit too easy going to me."

Bilal looked at his friend and comrade somewhat surprised by the question. Bilal and Ekrem were both from the ancient seaside village of Assos and had been conscripted into the Ottoman army at the same time. They missed home and hated their current posting in Arbanasi, although both would have to concede that things had improved since the previous Sanjakbey had been relocated.

"I find him alright," replied Bilal, "Although I haven't seen much of him. At least he leaves us alone, unlike the other bastard."

Ekrem looked thoughtful. He had obviously asked the question for a purpose.

"Well, yes, he leaves us alone alright, but that's just it," he mused. "Since he came the place has gone to the dogs. There's no discipline whatsoever. We already knew that our garrison commander was a lazy sod, but since the new Sanjakbey took over he does even less and everyone takes their lead from him. The place has become a shambles."

Although Bilal and Ekrem were good friends, as soldiers they were quite different. Whereas Ekrem took the job seriously Bilal just wanted a quiet life and the lazy commander who required very little from his men suited him just fine.

"I'm sure it doesn't matter one way or the other," Bilal maintained. "As long as you let them pray to their God, they're not bothered about anything else. Also you have to admit the girls here look better than any of the old boilers back at home. I notice that the Sanjakbey's son has been sniffing round them. Maybe we will get a turn," he suggested with a grin.

"I am afraid you are kidding yourself there, my friend," Ekrem assured him. "They all hate us, the men and the women. Believe me, they would slit our throats at the first opportunity and the way this camp is run it wouldn't be difficult."

Bilal tried to laugh off what his friend was saying, but deep down he knew there was some sense in it. There was a reason why good soldiers strived to maintain discipline and just for a moment Bilal started to feel vulnerable. However, when evening arrived and the jug of rakia was being passed around he forgot all about his conversation with his over earnest comrade.

*

Todor tried to pass over how Vasil Kolev and the other elders had come to know about their plans, but his comrades were having none of it.

"I just don't understand," protested Strahil "How does Kolev know? Surely no one has spoken to him about the planned resistance."

Todor continued with the same line. "It no longer matters how he knows, simply that he does."

"Well it matters to me!" Strahil persisted. "If we have a traitor in our midst, I want to know who it is."

"I told him."

Vladislav had never wanted Todor to protect him and now by doing so he had possibly weakened his own position. All eyes turned on Vladislav who continued amongst rising hostility from his erstwhile friends.

"I told him, but I am no traitor. I have been foolish, so foolish, but I am no traitor. If you want me to leave I will."

"Leave? You should be facing execution for treason. It is only because our so called leader is your friend that you are sitting here at all. You should be lying in a shallow grave with your throat cut," retorted Strahil.

"This has got to stop." Angel rarely spoke at meetings, but now he was fired up. "Listen to yourself, Strahil. You sound like a Turk. You have known Vladislav all your life and now you talk of slitting his throat like he were a rabid dog. If we start to turn on each other then we are no better than them."

There was muttering among the group and Strahil got to his feet. Todor glared at him.

"Sit down, Strahil, unless you are intending to take my place."

Strahil stared back with insolence in his eyes, but in his heart he knew he would never carry the group against Todor. Reluctantly and wordlessly he sat down again.

Danail was the next to speak. "Let's try and keep this civilised, can we? It would help us, Vladislav, if you told us all exactly what happened."

Vladislav told the sorry tale of how in a moment of weakness he had spoken to Kolev. Throughout he berated himself again and again. At the end he said that he was now aware that Kolev had spoken to his old friends and that it had now got out of hand in a way he had never foreseen. However, he maintained that Vasil Kolev and the people Kolev had spoken to were loyal Bulgarians.

"We are talking about our own fathers here. I do not believe it will go any further."

Todor was still not sure. "Has anyone any reason to believe that the information has gone further?"

"Yes," said Strahil "Kolev himself may be loyal, but what about his two stuck up daughters? Twice I have seen the young one speaking to the son of the Sanjakbey and yesterday her bitch of a sister was in long conversation with him. My mother saw them together."

"Don't be absurd! They are two people we could always rely on," said Vladislav, his temper rising.

"You are blind, Vladislav. We all know you are in love with the Turk's little whore."

In a flash Vladislav had Strahil by the throat and was about to strike him when his friends dragged him off.

"Enough!" yelled Todor. "I have decided the matter myself. The truth is we do not now know how far this has gone. We are no longer safe. We could all be dragged from our beds in the middle of the night by Turkish soldiers. We were almost ready so we will strike now."

"But, Todor, we cannot act until Rostislav Stratimirovic gives the order," Danail replied, no doubt speaking for most of his comrades.

"Stratimirovic is not even in the country," said Todor firmly. "I am in charge here and I say we strike."

Vladislav felt desperate. It was his fault entirely that they were being rushed into action, but he realised that as things stood they could all be arrested before they had even spilled a drop of Turkish blood. Angel spoke his thoughts.

"You are right, Todor. We are behind you."

All the others, even Strahil, immediately voiced their assent.

Speaking to each friend in turn, Todor asked all of them how many men they could muster. It appeared that from Arbanasi and the surrounding villages they could rely on close to three hundred men.

"It is not enough," exclaimed Todor. "I will go to Tarnovo and tell the others that all their men are to be mobilised. I think we could expect another thousand or so then, maybe more. I will go tonight and by the end of tomorrow I would have spoken to each and every one. We will meet again the day after tomorrow at first light in Danail's smithy. Be ready!"

*

The following day Rayna was out working in the field shortly after sunrise. Boryana had given a favourable account of her meeting with Bayram and had expressed some faith in his ability to get his way. This reassured Rayna, but Boryana's confidence more than anything revealed her own inexperience in such matters. For example, she knew nothing of the custom of arranged marriages within the Islamic community and in truth had not even thought about the different religious backgrounds of the young lovers. Had she done, she would have realised what an impossible task she had set the young man. Boryana had told Bayram that her sister would be working in the field the following morning and so leaving nothing to chance Rayna had risen with the lark and made her way to the family vegetable plot to await his arrival. She had only been working, or at least trying to work, for about thirty minutes before she heard his horse approaching.

As Bayram approached from the east, horse and rider were framed by the sun rising behind them. It was as if they had appeared out of the sun itself. Bayram brought his steed to a gentle stop and dismounted with an athleticism that was by no means lost on Rayna. He landed facing her no more than a foot away. She greeted him nervously in her own language and he replied in his. He took half a step towards her so that she could feel his breath on her forehead. It was not just that words no longer seemed to matter, they actually seemed inadequate. Rayna fought to keep control of her senses, but as he gently bent to kiss her, the floodgates of her emotions opened and, closing her eyes she offered her lips to him. She offered her whole self to him and he received her gratefully. All thoughts about family loyalties and worlds colliding were lost in one moment of love.

That afternoon Vladislav sat alone on the old bench outside his father's home. His task for the afternoon was to mind the family's small herd of goats while they grazed, but in warm weather they needed very little looking after being content to just snooze in the sun. This was just as well because Vladislav's mind was not really on the job. He had been thinking through the events of the last few days and had also been thinking about the planned assault on the Turkish soldiers. Like most of his comrades he knew in his heart that any success they might have would probably be short lived. Although there were no more than fifteen hundred Turkish troops in the Tarnovo region, the Ottoman army was a vast fighting machine with hundreds of thousands of men at their disposal. The only hope of success was if others from the rest of Bulgaria and beyond heard about their offensive and followed suit. If not they were all dead men. He knew therefore that the attempts by Rostislav Stratimirovic to find allies was crucial and also that by forcing Todor into an early offensive he had compromised Stratimirovic's efforts. However, the realisation that they could well be facing death did not deter Vladislav or his comrades. Better to die fighting for liberty than to live under the yoke of Turkish tyranny.

Soon enough Vladislav's thoughts turned to Rayna. His temper flared again as he thought about the outrageous things that Strahil had said about Rayna and her sister. Nevertheless, he did wonder what Boryana had been talking to the Turk about, if this part of Strahil's story could be relied upon. Vladislav still needed to speak urgently with Rayna and he realised that after tomorrow he may never see her again. He resolved to call on her there and then.

All of a sudden Vladislav was in a desperate hurry to see Rayna. He herded the reluctant goats into a small pen and without his father's prior permission he took the old man's horse from the field where she was grazing and set off towards Rayna's family home. Looking up at the sun he realised that there was still two hours of light left and so, changing course, he headed for the field where he felt sure she would still be working. As he got closer to the field he slowed his father's mare to a gentle trot. Vladislav leaned forward and patted her affectionately on the neck and as he looked up he saw another rider approaching him. It did not take him long to realise it was the young Turk. He was twisted in the saddle, looking back to where Rayna stood on the path and so at first he did not notice Vladislav approaching. Vladislav's heart sank as he saw the look of longing on Rayna's face as she watched Bayram riding away on the handsome Arab. His heart sank, but his blood boiled with hatred towards the Turk.

"Damn him, damn the bastard!" he cursed.

Dragging his eyes away from Rayna Bayram turned and found himself looking straight at Vladislav. They were by then only ten feet apart. According to the law Christians had to dismount from their horse when a Muslim passed the other way. Bayram sat on his horse waiting for the native boy to dismount to allow him to pass. Vladislav certainly had no intention of complying with this or any other law imposed by the Ottoman authorities.

"This is Bulgarian soil, Turk, stand aside!"

Hearing this, Rayna came forward and implored him to do as the law required.

"Vladislav, don't be a fool! Get off the horse or you will only find yourself in trouble."

Bayram sat still in the saddle and looked at him expectantly. In answer, Vladislav drove his horse forward and, pulling Bayram's leg violently from the stirrup tossed him to the ground. The young man fell awkwardly and appeared to be in considerable pain. Rayna let out an involuntary scream and ran to him to see how badly he was hurt.

"Vlado, what have you done?" she cried.

"May he and his accursed family rot in hell!" he replied.

Vladislav looked at Bayram with contempt as he writhed on the ground. Unconcerned as to the Turk's welfare he squeezed his legs against the mare's flanks and without a backward glance galloped away.

As he got closer to home, Vladislav realised that yet again he had allowed his temper to get the better of him. This time the consequences could be disastrous. Not thinking for one moment that Rayna would try and persuade the son of the Sanjakbey not to take action, he returned his father's horse to the paddock and headed for the forest where he intended to remain until first light. He just hoped that his foolish and rash behaviour would not bring trouble upon his family. But Rayna was his true friend and despite her anger at him she would not allow Bayram to leave her until he had promised on her life not to report Vladislav to the authorities. Given Bayram's position as the son of the local ruler, she knew that the punishment would be severe.

Bayram rode home at a snail's pace. His arm ached where he had fallen and his head, which had jolted backwards from the force of him hitting the ground, was pounding. His clothes and body were covered in the grey dust from the road. Above all he felt humiliated. Rayna had

been anxious that he should swear on her life that Vladislav would not
be reported to the authorities. She need not have worried. Bayram did
not need his father's soldiers to play any part in this matter. He would
deal with Vladislav Petrov himself and the next time the stupid peasant
would not be aided by the element of surprise. He would learn that
picking a fight with a young Turkish man was an extremely unwise
thing to do.

*

Todor rode back from Tarnovo feeling pleased with his day's
work. It was a beautiful ride with some of the most delightful scenery
in the entire region. When about half way home Todor brought his
horse to a halt and turned her round to look down upon the enchanting
city of Tarnovo. It was a splendid sight set amongst the hills with the
imposing River Yantra curling through and around it. Todor loved his
country and wanted nothing more than to live here in peace, unfettered
by the demands of a foreign power. He had no understanding of what
drove men beyond their own borders to lay claim to other people's
lands. He desired only to be left alone to enjoy the countryside that God
in his wisdom had set him down in, but if God had decreed that this
land belonged to the Bulgarian people he was prepared to fight to the
death if necessary to defend it.

Todor had spoken to the other local leaders with an air of authority
which had caused them to heed his words and agree to his plan. Like
him they were concerned that they were about to take up arms without
the order coming from Stratimirovic himself, but they were convinced
by Todor's argument that it would be dangerous to wait. A courier was
dispatched on their best horse to try and get word to their leader, but
they all knew that the assault would be over before the courier reached
him. The plan was that Todor's group would attack the small garrison
near Arbanasi believing that this would cause the Turkish commanders
to send troops from the city to quell the rebellion there. The partisans
from in and around Tarnovo would then attack the weakened
compound in the city. If things went well they could even be in control
of the region by nightfall.

The following morning before the sun had risen a furtive figure
could be seen entering the local church, cursing the creaking door as
he did so. From the outside, the bare stone walls of the church did not
reveal anything of the splendid colours and religious drama inside.
Separated into several sections the church was a maze of low ceilings

and thick walls. Each room of the interior was covered with scenes from the Old Testament mingled with solemn saints and poignant episodes from the Gospels. In the least decorated section of the church the icon of the Virgin Mary was displayed.

All his life Vladislav had been lucky, but suddenly everything seemed to be unravelling. If Todor had managed to persuade the other local leaders that the time for action had arrived then later that day there would be bloodshed. If the attack on the Turks was premature and not properly prepared for then a lot of Bulgarian blood would be spilled and it would be his fault. Also he had suspected and now it had been confirmed that Rayna, who he loved dearly, was intent on giving her heart to another. To make the bitter pill even harder to swallow for Vladislav the man she appeared to be infatuated with was an enemy of the Bulgarian people. He took the icon from its place and held it to him mouthing a silent prayer.

"God be with us!" he whispered.

Vladislav left the church with a grim expression and headed for the smithy.

Chapter Three

Danail had been an apprentice to his father and had then worked alongside him until a year ago when ill health had forced the older man to pass the smithy on to his son. He missed working with his father, but was nevertheless secretly proud when people in the village started to refer to the old place as Danail's Smithy. Like his comrades he was ready to do his duty in the fight to rid Bulgaria of the Turkish forces, but the impending fight weighed heavily upon him as it was he that now supported the family. He was striving to introduce his younger brother into a trade that had provided for their family for centuries, but he needed time. It could not be helped. For the time being he must put all this aside and concentrate on the forthcoming battle.

Todor stood by the anvil that was the focal point of the smithy to address his small band of men. Although he was only speaking to twelve men each of them had others that they could bring to the fight and so they represented around three hundred loyal Bulgarians, most of whom Todor had known all of his life. By the end of the day some of the young men looking up at him would be dead and possibly many others too. He knew that his plan held more danger for his troops than for any others. He did not anticipate great difficulty in taking the small garrison at Arbanasi. They were few in number and would not be expecting a strike. What is more, from what he had observed they were getting lazy showing more interest in lying about in the sun with a jug of rakia than behaving like soldiers. The new Sanjakbey was a more decent man than his predecessor, but although a military man himself he did not seem to put the fear of God into his soldiers as the last Sanjakbey had done and things had become more lax. The danger would occur after the attack on the small Arbanasi garrison which was essentially a decoy meant to draw the main Turkish forces away from the city. If the Turks reacted as he anticipated this would mean a massive force being sent from Tarnovo to crush the uprising at Arbanasi. His men could then become overwhelmed.

Todor knew that if he shared these concerns with his men they would elect to carry on anyway, but as a commander he had to recognise the difference between bravery and recklessness. These were good men, as good as any others throughout Bulgaria. Each of them would willingly give his life in the cause of victory and freedom, but he did not want to see any one of them fall needlessly. It was his responsibility to see that this did not happen. It was a responsibility that weighed heavily upon him.

As he addressed his men his mind was working overtime trying to think of a solution, some way of keeping at least most of his men safe. However, he had overlooked the fact that he was not the only member of the group with the ability to think strategically. As Todor outlined the plan Vladislav too had worked out that this was potential suicide for the men of Arbanasi. Vladislav indicated that he wanted to speak and Todor was only too glad to give the floor to someone else.

"Todor, I understand your plan. It is a good plan, probably the only way that we are likely to be successful, but we can all see that it presents great risks to us and our men."

"What! Are you afraid to die for your country?" Strahil shouted.

"Let him finish, Strahil," commanded Todor.

"No, I am not afraid to die," continued Vladislav, "In fact I expect it, and I know that I carry a great burden of guilt that we are being forced to act now, possibly prematurely."

"Vladislav that does not matter now," said Angel in support of his friend.

"Oh, but it does matter, Angel. It matters a great deal," replied Vladislav.

He was not seeking forgiveness that he did not believe he deserved.

"Once we have taken the garrison here in Arbanasi we can throw any Turks who are left alive into their own stinking prison," said Vladislav, "Once that is achieved there is no need for all of us to remain here. We only need enough men to convince the Turkish troops from the city that their garrison at Arbanasi is under our control and of course to hold out as long as possible to keep them from the city. It would be a better use of the rest of the Arbanasi forces to join their comrades at Tarnovo. What happens here is of lesser importance. Tarnovo is the key. I will stay with my small troop of fifty. That will be enough."

The room fell silent. Even Strahil was lost for words. In the face of such bravery there was little to be said, but Todor was the first to speak.

"Vladislav, it is a brave gesture that you make, but I, we cannot allow this. We will remain together."

"What, and die together?" retorted Vladislav. "It is a waste of good men."

Every man in the room knew that Vladislav spoke sense. They looked at Todor expectantly.

"Maybe you are right, Vladislav, but if that is what we should do it will be me that stays," said Todor firmly.

"Old friend," began Vladislav, "In the absence of Rostislav Stratimirovic you are the leader of this fight. The other local commanders as well as your own men are looking to you for guidance. No, it will be me that holds the garrison. My mind is made up."

Vladislav's demeanour made it clear that the discussion was now at an end.

As the men left the room Strahil approached Vladislav and offered his hand. Strahil was a fanatically patriotic Bulgarian and hated all Turks without exception. He saw the world in black and white and rarely questioned his own judgements, but on this occasion he could see that he had been wrong.

"Please forgive my foolish words, comrade. I had no right to judge you so harshly. If any of the men in this room live through this day they will have you to thank. Whatever happens, we will all be forever in your debt."

"There is nothing to forgive." said Vladislav simply.

The twelve men left the smithy with no further exchange of words. They all knew their solemn duty and each went to prepare their men for the battle ahead, some like Angel and Danail with a heavy heart; others like Strahil with the fervour of the impending battle burning inside them.

*

Within an hour of the garrison at Arbanasi falling to the local rebel army, word of it had reached Tarnovo. The Sanjakbey, Bayram's father, was irritated rather than anxious. He called one of his captains to him and gave him very clear orders.

"Take two platoons to Arbanasi and retake the garrison there. If he is still alive I want the garrison commander brought before me. What were they doing there? Sleeping, no doubt."

The captain was not sure that the Sanjakbey's orders were sound.

"Sir, I believe the garrison was attacked by some three hundred men. Two platoons may not be sufficient."

The Sanjakbey's irritation rose further.

"If you need a whole battalion to see off a few hundred farm boys with pick handles as weapons then take a damn battalion. Just make sure you wipe them out and remember, I want that idiot of a commander brought here."

The captain bit his tongue, but his pride had been pricked by the Sanjakbey's words. He did not need a whole battalion that consisted of nearly seven hundred men, but equally he had no intention of finding himself short of soldiers and unable to complete the task. He would take a battalion and get the job done quickly.

As soon as Bayram heard that soldiers were being despatched to Arbanasi he began to worry about Rayna and her sister. Once the garrison had been reclaimed the soldiers would be looking for some entertainment and he knew only too well what that meant. When his father complained idly about the captain who was to take charge of the operation, he saw his opportunity.

"Father, if you do not trust him then let me go with him to see that he carries out his duty effectively. I will be glad of the chance to honour your name."

The Sanjakbey was surprised, but pleased that his son was taking an interest in military matters. However, he did not want him getting killed.

"Yes, go with him, but do not get involved in the fighting. Try and find out who is behind this outrage. You will be of more use to me doing that."

Bayram readily agreed and the Sanjakbey sent word to the captain that his son would be accompanying him. The captain received the news with bitterness. As the son of the Sanjakbey Bayram would automatically outrank him and this he found irksome.

It had not taken any great effort for Todor and his men to take control of the garrison at Arbanasi. The garrison was very badly guarded and they had been able to approach unseen. Many of the soldiers seemed to be sleeping off hangovers from the previous evening's drinking bout and others were just sitting around in small groups enjoying the early morning sun.

"So much for the invincible Ottoman army!" observed Todor to his friends.

A large number of the enemy had been slain, although the majority were now incarcerated in their own filthy prisons. Strahil, as well as others, had pointed out to Todor that keeping prisoners constituted an unnecessary danger. Todor knew this to be so, but what was the point of freeing your community of Turkish oppression and immediately behaving in the same brutal manner. He was not prepared to see the soldiers wantonly slain and was able to resist the calls of Strahil and his supporters. As planned, Vladislav was to be left in charge and despite the danger posed by the prisoners he too had no stomach for mass slaughter.

Inside one of the small and filthy cells Bilal sat on the floor with ten other Turkish soldiers. Outside their Bulgarian captors appeared to be discussing whether they should live or die. Bilal and the other soldiers expected to be executed. In such a situation the Turks would not have hesitated to put all the captives to the sword. Although Bilal's friend Ekrem had foreseen something like this happening it had not helped him when the attack came. Ekrem's lifeless body lay just ten metres away with his skull crushed by an iron shovel. One of the Turkish soldiers in the cell had been shaking with fear and had now started to snivel and wail. His comrades found it intolerable and shouted at him to be quiet. When he did not respond an older battle hardened soldier picked up his own helmet and struck the younger man a savage blow across his uncovered head. He fell to the floor unconscious, blood oozing from the wound. His comrades looked on unmoved, just grateful that he was at last quiet. If they were going to be slain they at least wanted to face death in peace and with some dignity.

When the time came Todor remained reluctant to leave his brave friend behind, but he knew well enough that his duty lay elsewhere and with little delay he took the larger part of his force onto the road to Tarnovo. After forty minutes they could see the city nestling below them, its small dwelling houses hanging on the edge of the steep banks of the river Yantra. It looked so peaceful that for a moment Todor doubted the whole enterprise, but of course he knew that the apparent peace currently settling across the city was an illusion. The truth was that the people of this city and others across Bulgaria were subject to a tyrannical oppression by a merciless foreign power. His cause was good and with this thought sustaining him he upped his pace, marching his small but valiant band boldly towards the city and the battle ahead.

Two of the party, Danail and Angel, were deep in conversation trying to sustain each other for what was to come.

"I have worked so hard trying to get my brother trained up as a farrier, but I just haven't had the time I needed. He is willing enough, but Kiril is a slow learner. If anything happens to me my family will face a perilous future." said Danail, his anxiety showing in his face.

"Nothing will happen to you, Danail. God and justice will prevail." replied Angel.

Danail looked at him hard. "Even if justice does prevail some of us will pay for it with our lives. We both know that."

Angel knew that what his friend said was true, but he was trying to be philosophical as well as brave. As they walked on Angel put his arm around his friend's shoulders.

"What can we do, Danail? Our cause is just and we must fight for our freedom. There is no other way. If we die we will at least die proudly."

In response Danail puffed out his chest and quickened his stride, nodding his assent.

Suddenly Todor's small group of rebels found the battle coming to them. Just fifteen minutes away from entering Tarnovo they confronted the Turkish force that had been mobilised to liberate the garrison at Arbanasi. Todor could see at a glance that he was considerably outnumbered and although his men had acquired some weaponry from the defeated garrison he could safely assume that the Turks were armed to the teeth. Todor acted quickly and decisively sending two runners to summon help. One went back to the garrison to inform Vladislav and the other was despatched to Arbanasi village to find anyone who was prepared to fight. He then ordered his men to retreat to a rocky outcrop four hundred metres back in the hope that they could hold that position until help arrived.

The messenger reached Arbanasi very quickly and his plea for help spread like wildfire around the village. His request did not go unheeded and soon a large group of older men, many of them fathers of the stranded soldiers, and an almost as large group of young women armed with anything from clubs to gardening implements were following the messenger down the hill towards Tarnovo. Almost simultaneously word reached Vladislav. Leaving just five men to guard the prisoners he and his small band of followers set off in the same direction, relieved that the tension of waiting for the attack to come to them was finally over.

Rayna, Boryana and their father were amongst the villagers who had responded to the call. Vasil Kolev and his elder daughter Boryana were quite clear about what they were doing and why they were ready to join the fight against the Turks. All through their lives Vasil had tried to talk to his daughters about freedom and justice and the need to rid themselves of their Turkish oppressors. Boryana had always listened eagerly and now shared many of her father's views. Rayna on the other hand had never really picked up on her father's message. She was more interested in the natural world and did not really understand why others concerned themselves so much about their differences. To Rayna the world was a lovely place for everyone to enjoy equally. As she drew closer to the place where the young men were fighting for their lives it occurred to her for the first time that Bayram could be amongst the Turkish forces. How stupid and naïve had she been? As the son of the local lord it was inevitable that he would be there. Rayna had joined the group out of loyalty to her father and to her friends. She had grown up with these young men and they needed help. For her that had been enough. Now suddenly her whole world was considerably more complicated. All at once she was afraid.

For some time Todor and his men managed to hold the Turks at bay, but by the time the villagers arrived on the scene a full scale battle had commenced. Bayram was in the thick of it despite his father's orders to the contrary. As they drew close the villagers let out an almighty cry and surged forward. The sheer numbers sent fear and trepidation through the Turkish ranks as the odds suddenly changed dramatically. Looking up Bayram was shocked to see Rayna and her sister to the fore of the group and from fearing for his own life his concerns shifted dramatically to focus on the girl he had fallen in love with. He hardly had time to think because seconds later a smaller but more menacing force of Bulgarian rebels emerged from behind the rocks that their comrades had been defending. Unlike the main Bulgarian force who only had clubs and homemade swords this second group were armed with Turkish weapons that had been taken from the soldiers at the Arbanasi garrison including maces, daggers and yataghans with their short pointed blades. Out in front was the young man that had thrown him from his horse and soon it became clear to Bayram that the man's eyes were focused unerringly on him.

Soon Vladislav, assuming the son of the Sanjakbey was in command of the Turkish force, was running along the path towards him. Bayram stepped onto the path to meet his charge. As he stepped out Rayna saw him for the first time and her heart froze. Then almost in the same instant she saw Vladislav. Some unknown force seemed to take her over and before she had time to think she was on her feet, running, undeterred by the danger around her. She had no clear idea of her own purpose as her mind struggled with the contradictory forces of love and loyalty. In no time the two men were locked in combat. Rayna screamed. She called in vain for help. She knew not whose help she was trying to summon. On she ran unaware of what she intended to do. Although driven by fear and dread it was love that drew her to them, two different types of love. On the one hand a love born from a lifetime of familiarity, a loyal love based on a shared past; on the other hand a passionate all-consuming love with no base at all but stronger than any other. Her heart was beating so loud surely they would both hear it and draw back for her sake. But male pride had taken over. So intent were they on each other's destruction they had not even seen her.

Back amongst the group of villagers Rayna's father suddenly realised his youngest daughter was no longer by his side. He looked frantically about him and finally saw her rushing to where two men were fighting slightly away from the main site of the battle. The Bulgarian, who he now recognised as Vladislav Petrov, was armed with a short bladed sword and the young Turk was wielding a mace. As the old man looked on Vladislav was pushed to the ground and the Turk seemed about to crack his foe's head open.

At that moment he heard a voice ring out. With a feeling of dread he recognised the voice as that of his daughter.

"No! Please, no!" she yelled.

As the young Turkish soldier looked round she lunged herself at him from behind not knowing what she hoped to achieve. With the weight of her body upon him Bayram lost his balance and falling forward he was impaled on Vladislav's sword. For a lesser man the death may well have been instant, but Bayram fought for life, for the life he had imagined with this girl. By now Rayna's father and her sister Boryana were rushing towards the scene. Rayna, although she had saved the life of her friend, now looked not to Vladislav, but flung herself on the ground before the bleeding body of the young Turkish soldier and wept copiously. With the last of his strength Bayram stretched out his arm and lifted Rayna's face so they could look at each other one more time.

"It is not the end. I know it cannot be the end." he whispered and in that moment he died with his eyes still wide open taking Rayna's beauty with him to the grave.

Her father looked on bewildered. He turned at last to his elder daughter Boryana for some sort of explanation. Boryana dropped her head and between her own silent tears answered her father's unspoken questions.

"You told her, father, you told her never to forget she was Bulgarian."

*

With the son of the Sanjakbey dead and their captain also mortally wounded the Turkish soldiers, now leaderless and outnumbered, turned and fled back to the city. Behind them they left a scene of carnage with the dead and dying from both sides strewn across the hillside. Todor led his troops in pursuit anticipating that he would there meet up with the partisans that the other local leaders had at their command. Todor was at the front of his group of soldiers, but was the whole time looking back ticking off his friends in his mind, trying to establish who might have fallen. Sadly he had himself witnessed the death of Angel and this made him profoundly sad. Angel had been a true and loyal comrade who had given his life on the field of battle without a thought for himself. Todor had always regarded Angel as particularly brave because he was not naturally inclined to fight. He had reached the decision to join the struggle because he believed in it in spite of his reluctance to spill the blood of others. Maybe this was why he now lay dead. Had that distaste of killing caused him to hesitate at the vital moment? Todor shuddered at the thought of having to speak to Angel's parents, people he had known and admired since childhood. He would have to steel himself. Before the day was done there would be many more mothers and fathers waiting in vain for the return of their son.

Most troubling to him was his inability to account for the whereabouts of his friend, Vladislav. Strahil had reported the clash between Vladislav and the Turk and was quite clear that, thanks to Rayna, he had survived. Strahil had described what he had seen with feelings of shame given what he had said about Rayna and her sister just a couple of days earlier. Todor did nothing to relieve him of his guilt. If you speak of good people so loosely you should have to suffer the consequences of the injustices you deal out. So if his friend had lived, where was he now? In his heart Todor feared that Strahil had not witnessed the encounter to the end.

In fact his friend Vladislav was indeed still alive as Strahil had reported. He had remained with Rayna and her father and sister by the young man's body. Boryana had her arm tightly around her young sister in an attempt to comfort her, but it was of no use. They sat in still silence as if paralysed. Rayna, her face wholly drained of colour, just looked blankly at Bayram lying on the ground before her unable to take in what had happened. Vladislav looked on and could see the meaning of it all and the enormity of Rayna's love for the fallen soldier. He realised there was no place for him here and no room in Rayna's heart to celebrate his survival. Slowly he stood and walked mournfully away. Rayna had loved the young Turk so deeply and yet had found herself compelled to end that love for the sake of her country and her friend. As she sat in the arms of her sister staring at the body in a pool of blood that she herself had spilt, she felt that her life too was over.

Vladislav walked slowly into the church. His life was saved, but his heart was broken. He approached the icon of the Virgin Mary that until now he believed had brought him good fortune. Solemnly he took the icon from its perch. Now with more purpose to his step he left the church and headed into the hills near his home. Presently he arrived at the place where he had first uncovered the icon and where his father had told him of the legend. With little ceremony Vladislav dug a deep hole and wrapping the icon in his shirt he buried it in the very spot where he had found it.

*

At Arbanasi later that day there was wild rejoicing. Already buoyed by the sight of the beaten battalion of Turkish soldiers retreating, word had now reached the villagers that Todor's forces, together with the partisan army assembled in the city, were locked in battle with the main Turkish force in Tarnovo. Everyone in the village felt sure they would prevail. At least in this moment they felt wonderfully free of oppression.

Somehow Rayna, supported by her sister and father, had made it back to the village. Her intention, as far as she had intentions, was to slip quietly into her home and shut herself in the small room that she and her sister shared as their sleeping quarters. Entering the village she could instantly see that celebrations were taking place, the last thing she would have wanted, but soon it became clear that in particular her return had been eagerly awaited. The villagers regarded her as a heroine and gathered jubilantly around her making it almost impossible for her to pass. She was horror struck, and although her sister and father did their best to discourage attention, her friends and relatives could not be held back. Even those young women that usually ignored her, jealous of her beauty, seemed to have reviewed their opinion of her and the young men looked upon her with even more admiration than before. Suddenly there was a short pause when Rayna stared back with such a ghostlike expression, her face white and vacant, that her admirers were for a few seconds hesitant, unable to comprehend her reaction. Her sister, her best friend in the world, seized the moment and bustled her sister forward and into their home at the same time giving out the news that Rayna was exhausted and needed some time to recover. The throng were disappointed, but Boryana was not someone they were accustomed to arguing with. Reluctantly they withdrew and when one amongst them revealed a bottle of rakia from under his coat they resumed their celebrations.

Sitting alone Rayna could hear her family discussing her plight in respectful whispers whilst outside the celebrations continued unabated. She had no idea how she would face the next few hours let alone the next few days and weeks. She had developed from a girl to a woman in a matter of a few days, maybe in a matter of moments. She was only eighteen and had her whole life still to lead. Just a short time ago she felt sure that every moment would be precious, now the life ahead of her seemed like a curse. Whatever else, she knew that in this life she would never love again. Her love for Bayram had brought her such joy, but this had now slipped away to be replaced by a deep melancholy. Nevertheless, despite everything, she hoped this was a love from which she would never recover.

Part Two

Arbanasi
Present Day

Chapter Four

At eighteen Vladimir had certainly had a fine set of teeth and it could be said that this was the best feature of a generally handsome face. Now more than fifteen years later he was no longer so proud of his teeth and had long since given up the rather vain habit of making sure they were visible on the rare occasions that he smiled. The deterioration, which was nowhere near as bad as he thought, was due to a combination of bad diet, a temper that was bigger than him and a lack of funds to pay for dental work. Now that he was a bit better off a dentist, if he should choose to visit one, would still have plenty to work with. As for his other features they still largely retained the promise of his youth although his mouth was always turned down denoting a melancholy that should not yet have settled upon a man of just thirty five.

He was now by Bulgarian standards earning quite well and for this he had his English neighbour Tim to thank. For twelve months now Vladimir had been the proud owner of an old transit van and although he had bought it in order to do transport jobs, for the first nine months he had acquired very few commissions. Had it not been for the fact that Tim was slowly furnishing his house and needed things collecting, he and his old van would hardly have worked at all.

About three months ago he had collected a sofa for Tim from a local second hand shop and it was on the way home that Tim put the idea into his head.

"These bloody shops in this country drive me mad," Tim had complained, "They sell furniture and yet they have no means of delivering it. It is just the same if you go to buy a fridge, a stove or a washing machine. Do you do transport? Ne! Haven't they got any sense? Not everyone has a bleedin' van or a trailer. Why don't they find some local fella with a van and contact him when a customer wants something moving? Someone like you, Vlado. It would be perfect for you. Man with a Van, we call it in the UK. You could clean up!"

Vladimir had taken Tim at his word. However in typical Bulgarian style he had first of all wasted the little bit of savings he had on having his van professionally sign written. This was in any event unnecessary, but was even more of a waste of money given that he had chosen to have it done in English. 'Vladimir - Man with a Van' it proclaimed proudly. Unfortunately, only Tim could understand it and he already knew. Unperturbed Vladimir had put the second part of Tim's plan into action and had visited every second hand shop, furniture store and white goods retailers in the nearby town leaving his contact details and declaring himself open for business. The take up had been immediate and within a few weeks Vladimir had as much work as he wanted. Tim was pleased for him, the only downside being that Vladimir was now not always available when Tim wanted him.

Tim and his wife Margot had first come to Bulgaria on holiday in 2005. They had stayed at a resort near Varna. The weather had been glorious, the coastline was lovely and everything was so cheap. They had really enjoyed themselves. Why wouldn't they? On returning home they had made some preliminary enquiries about property in Bulgaria with a vague notion that they might like a holiday retreat somewhere near the coast. People had said that property prices were very low. At first they had been looking at coastal apartments which, compared to say Spain, were cheap, but still beyond what Tim and Margot could sensibly afford. Margot had forgotten all about it, but Tim had been like a dog with a bone and had continued looking. Eventually he had found himself looking on the internet at villages inland and he could not believe what was available.

Tim tried hard to get Margot engaged again, but having failed to realise her dream of a seaside apartment she had no real interest in a three bedroom house miles from the coast with no electricity and no running water. Tim's assertion that it would be a great investment cut no ice with her even if houses could be bought for two thousand pounds. Tim should have left it there, but he just couldn't bring himself to give it up.

Tim and Margot had been married since they were no more than kids and they had reached a point where they felt totally comfortable with each other. Sometimes over a bottle of wine and a few glasses of beer they would chat for hours, other times they would sit reading or doing some small jobs around the house and hardly speak. Both of them were happy either way. The key to their relationship was complete openness with each other. So when Tim secretly dipped into their small savings and purchased an old house near the town of Veliko Tarnovo, he broke every unspoken rule that they lived by. That would have been bad enough, but to compound the felony he bought it unseen from the internet.

When they met Tim had been working for a small landscaping and groundwork company driving a digger. He was starting to get frustrated with the small minded way in which the owner ran the business and had recently decided to try and buy a digger himself and set up on his own. On their first date Tim had memorably spent half the evening telling Margot about his plans and also confided that he was still hopelessly short of the money required for the digger. On his way home he realised how uncool he had been.

"God, the poor girl must have been bored to death." he told himself as he made his way through the familiar unlit lanes that led to his parents' house.

Two days later Tim was overwhelmed with anxiety when he rang Margot to ask if he could see her again. He was sure she would say no, but to his relief she not only agreed, but seemed very pleased that he had rung.

When they went out together on their second date Tim was determined to get it right. He chose a newly opened Indian restaurant in the nearby town and although he was forced to pick her up in his dad's van Margot still seemed really happy with the evening he had planned. As they walked into the restaurant Margot was fascinated by the décor which was mock-colonial, with bamboo chairs and an array of pictures showing Indian scenes hung on heavy flock wallpaper. Colourful hanging lamps adorned the ceiling and a large fish tank took pride of place in the centre of the restaurant. Piped music formed a discreet background entertainment, while waiters in bow ties moved noiselessly between the tables. Tim could see that she was impressed.

Tim felt ridiculously proud as he and Margot were shown to their table. The waiter came across, lit their candles and gave them each a menu.

"What would you like to drink?" he enquired.

"Should we have a bottle of white wine, Tim?" Margot asked.

"Yes, if that's what you want," he replied, his confidence growing. Then turning to the waiter he made his order.

"A bottle of house white," he said "And a pint of bitter, please."

Margot suppressed a smile. He was just so plain and honest. Margot knew she really liked him.

The waiter went off to fetch their drinks and Tim started to go through the menu, but Margot had something to say.

"Just leave that a minute," she implored looking at him quite intently. "I have something to ask you."

Tim lifted his eyes from the menu and returned her gaze. It turned out that Margot also had a couple of surprises for him.

"How much are you short for this digger you are wanting to buy?" she enquired.

Despite his promises to himself not to talk about this again, within seconds he was recounting the whole story of the narrow minded boss and his own ideas on how to run a business like this. Margot waited patiently for the answer to her question.

"The bank manager said he could lend me four thousand pounds if I could come up with one thousand myself, but it's hopeless. I only have between three and four hundred saved and all mum and dad can spare is about two hundred. I'll just have to forget it."

Margot looked him over seemingly coming to some sort of decision. She put her hand into her bag and pulled out a thick brown envelope.

"Perhaps this will help," she said simply. She pushed the envelope across the table. "There is four hundred and sixty there. It is all I have, but you are welcome to it."

Tim's jaw dropped open and he sat staring at her like an imbecile. "I, I can't take that. You hardly know me. Margot, that's a fortune."

"I know that," she replied. "I have been saving it since I was twelve!"

"But, Margot, it's just not possible."

"I'm not giving it away," she said, "There are two conditions."

"What? Anything," Tim mumbled.

"Firstly it has to be a JCB. My dad said all the others are nowhere near as good. And secondly, I want you to marry me." said Margot calmly. "….as soon as you have bought the digger."

Unfortunately Tim had just taken a deep draft of ale to try and calm his nerves and he spat half of it across the table.

"Shall I take that as a yes?" she asked.

"You're on!" was the best he could come up with.

Five weeks later they were married and they left the church in a brand new jointly owned yellow digger and with absolutely no secrets between them.

Now Tim had a secret from Margot, a great big secret at that, and it was weighing heavily upon him. He would have to tell her. As was Tim's way he chose his moment badly. Margot had just been going through their monthly finances and had concluded that they were not really making ends meet.

"I just don't understand it. I mean the business is doing really well, especially now we have the coal board contract. It's this bloody house that's taking all our money. The mortgage is ridiculous. I just don't know where we go from here."

So just when Margot was in a stew about money, Tim somehow decided that this was his moment to come clean.

"Well we could always move to our other house," he said with an inane grin on his face.

If he thought his revelation was going to be greeted with enthusiasm, he was very much mistaken.

"What are you on about?" Margot asked.

"The house I bought in Bulgaria, just in case we ever needed it." said Tim. "In a little village near.….."

"You what?"

Margot's stare was long and hard and as Tim wilted before her eyes, she turned on her heel and slammed the door as she charged out of the house.

"A little village near Veliko Tarnovo" Tim mournfully completed his sentence to himself as he watched his wife's back disappear through the door.

From that moment on there was a subtle change in their relationship and although Margot finally came to trust Tim again, she was always hyper alert whenever he started talking about some hare brained scheme. Of course, once the dust settled and Margot came to terms with being the owner of a house in Arbanasi, she obviously wanted to see it. Given he had purchased it on the internet she thought that Tim ought to see it too! Luckily for Tim, Margot loved the place. Arbanasi is actually one of the most beautiful villages in the region and the house, though in a poor state, was in the traditional Bulgarian renaissance style, apparently built in about 1820 on a site where there had been a house since about 1650.

Twice a year Tim and Margot visited the village for a working holiday and slowly they had introduced modern amenities without spoiling the character of the place. When they retired with Tim still only in his early fifties, they sold their UK house and moved to Arbanasi. They were happy.

Since moving to Bulgaria Margot had made a point of joining as many ex Pat groups on Facebook as she could find. Although she never posted anything herself, each evening she trawled through the pages of Facebook for about thirty minutes to see what was new. Every five minutes or so she shared a piece of news or information with Tim and each time his response was the same, basically that he did not give a toss. He had a couple of British friends with whom he shared an occasional pint and besides Vladimir one Bulgarian friend, Milen, who helped him whenever he had to confront Bulgarian bureaucracy. He had no interest in what the other eighteen thousand Brits in Bulgaria were getting up to. On this occasion, however, he showed a degree of interest in the information Margot was sharing with him.

"Tim, listen to this. You know you are always looking for a labourer-cum-handyman. Well there are people here that do it for nothing. Apparently lots of the Brits use them."

It was true that Tim had for some time been trying to find a Bulgarian who would work two or three days a week for cash. The going rate was about twenty five leva a day, less than ten pounds, but although many Bulgarians were out of work Tim only ever managed to get someone for the odd day here and there. When he spoke to them about regular work they either said they were not interested or agreed, but then did not turn up. He had in the end been forced to conclude that they did not like work. Although Margot maintained that it must be his fault in some way, Tim was not aware what he could do differently.

"What do you mean, for nothing? Nobody works for nothing. Most people here don't want the work even when you pay them."

Margot was reading and answering at the same time.

"It says here it is some kind of scheme. You register as a host, say what work you want doing and people apply to come and work for you. Students and the like."

Tim had never had the benefit of a university education, but he was certain that it did not equip students for grubbing around in a Bulgarian village in temperatures of thirty degrees plus.

"How many students do you know who can work hard?" Tim enquired.

"I don't know any students and nor do you," Margot retorted. "Anyway these people are from all over the world and they are not all students as far as I can make out. There are all sorts of people."

Tim got the name of the website from Margot and took a look himself. Although he was sceptical he thought it worth exploring. He soon discovered that the young people who were offering work would go online and choose a host from the website's listings. Each host gave basic details about themselves and their location and a description of the work they wanted doing. The very important bit that Margot had not picked up was that the person was required to live with the host for the duration of the work placement which could be for any length of time by agreement between the two parties. However, if you got someone you liked and he or she was a good worker it was overall a good deal. Looking at the details that the hosts had posted about themselves Tim wondered whether the dangers lay more with the potential workers. For example, the revelation by a couple who were seventy plus that they were naturists and likely be seen about the house and garden naked did not seem to Tim to be a particular recommendation. Being seen by a person of twenty odd with your crusty bits on show was in Tim's opinion not altogether decent, although Margot was certain they would be a great attraction. After some discussion during which Margot made some ridiculous and rather unseemly suggestions, they decided to give it a go. Tim undertook to make the application to be listed and see what came of it.

Tim wondered how to describe the work he was offering as it varied from day to day and was basically the jobs that he never seemed to get round to. He could not think how to make it sound attractive enough for anyone to want to come and work for them. 'The dross work that the owner doesn't fancy' was hardly likely to get people queuing up. However, as he read what other hosts had written he realised that this was less of a problem than he had feared. Most people had made entries like 'Gardening and work about the house' or 'Helping us do up our new home', either of which would aptly describe what Tim and Margot had on offer. In the end Tim settled for a degree of honesty and an attempt at humour that he thought people might like. 'The work in the house and garden that we can no longer ignore.' Margot thought it was neither clever nor funny, but given she could not be bothered to come up with anything better, Tim's entry stood.

The more Tim read about the scheme the more it became apparent that choices were made largely on the basis of location and here they had a lot to offer. Arbanasi was a beautiful and historic village famous for its ancient monasteries and much visited by foreign tourists. The nearby city of Veliko Tarnovo was possibly the most enchanting place in Bulgaria. Twenty minutes after Tim had submitted their details along with some photographs their listing went live. Predictably Margot, who had not taken the whole thing very seriously, immediately got cold feet.

"I don't want some bloke I have never met wandering around the place," she objected. "What if we get some weirdo?"

"Don't worry, they'll all be heading for the naturists," Tim retorted. "It's done now. If we don't like the look of someone who applies we can just say the placement is currently unavailable."

"You can't get rid of weirdos that easily!" Margot warned, but Tim, realising she was getting ridiculous again, ended the conversation with "We'll just have to wait and see."

Their wait would not be a long one.

*

Vladimir had been grateful for Tim's suggestion about the van, but now he was working harder than he had ever worked in his life and was finding little time to relax with his friends. He decided he needed an assistant and as is the Bulgarian way he first of all started enquiries within his family.

"What about your cousin Momchil?" his mother suggested. "He is always wanting work."

"Don't be silly mother. Momchil is blind, totally blind. How could he carry furniture?"

"You'll have to employ someone else to act as his eyes and guide him when he is carrying something," his mother said as if it was the obvious answer.

"In which case I might as well just employ someone that can see in the first place. The whole suggestion is ridiculous," Vladimir protested, but his mother was ready for him.

"His younger sister, Denitsa, is not in work either. You have seen her, she is so small and slim she could not carry heavy things, but she could act as guide to her brother."

It was true that Vladimir had seen his young cousin. She was in every way a joy to behold and on more than one occasion he had to remind himself that they were closely related. The girl was stunning.

"Anyway, mother, they live a hundred kilometres from here. The whole thing is impractical."

He hoped this would be the final word on the subject, but his mother was not done yet.

"It will be good for you, Vladimir. I worry about you rumbling around in that big house by yourself. You need some company and what better company is there than family?"

"I like being on my own, mother. Now let that be an end to it."

"It's not natural to want to be on your own," his mother said and so, knowing she would not relent he decided to walk away.

"It's not natural, I say!" she shouted after him.

Vladimir headed home to lick his wounds. "So much for asking my mother," he said to himself.

He would ask around at the village bar. Surely it was just as good to offer work to a neighbour as to a relative. His mouth started to water at the thought of some rakia and spicy sausage and so he decided there was no time like the present. He grabbed his coat that was still lying on the chair and headed for the door. As he was closing it behind him his mobile rang. Vladimir stared at the screen. It was not a number he recognised. It had never been his practice to answer the phone to a number he did not know, but since his man with a van business started he had by necessity had to change this policy. Fifty percent of his business calls were from unknown sources.

"Hello."

His heart sank. It was his Aunty Rada, the mother of Momchil and Denitsa.

"Vladimir, you are such a good boy. Your mother has given us the news. Momchil and Denitsa are thrilled. They are so looking forward to living and working with their rich cousin. You have made an old lady very happy."

Vladimir's aunt then started to cry with happiness. His aunt was even more manipulative than her sister, his own dear mother. Vladimir was beaten and he knew it.

*

Halim had never been to Bulgaria, although he had lived quite close to the Turkish/Bulgarian border for most of his life. His father had for the past year been the Turkish Consulate to Bulgaria based in the coastal city of Varna. According to his father, it was a beautiful country and Varna was a smart city that any young person would love. Halim had recently finished his history studies at Anadolu University and it was widely expected that he would follow in his father's footsteps and join the diplomatic service. Halim himself had no great objection to that plan. He loved and respected his father and greatly admired the work he did. However, before taking that step he wanted to create some independence for himself and so although he was interested in seeing Bulgaria he would not be heading for Varna. Also he did not want his father to pay for everything, although Halim knew his father would be happy and able to do this.

His best friend, Ayaz, had told him about a European scheme whereby you live with host families who give you accommodation and meals in exchange for work. Ayaz was currently working on a farm in Germany under this arrangement. Halim went online to see if the scheme operated in Bulgaria and was pleasantly surprised to see that it did, although it was noticeable that the majority of host families in Bulgaria were in fact English. In many ways this suited Halim. He was fluent in English and although he wanted to learn Bulgarian he would not be under pressure to try and speak it from the outset. He browsed through the list of hosts without really knowing what he was looking for, but when he got to the listing that Tim had posted he stopped looking any further. The work did not sound too demanding and the English couple sounded nice, but it was the location that particularly interested him.

Whilst studying history he had thoroughly researched the Ottoman Empire and, for reasons that were never quite clear to him, had become particularly interested in the period during which they ruled over Bulgaria. This host family lived near Veliko Tarnovo, the ancient capital of Bulgaria where two uprisings against Turkish rule had taken place. The second uprising had started in the nearby village of Arbanasi and Halim had gone to great lengths to find material about these events. However, the only source about the uprising was the family chronicles of the Rostislavov-Dubrovski clan. Many historians doubted its authenticity and considered it little more than 'a beautiful legend'. Nevertheless, the Ottoman archives did also speak of insurgent activities in the Tarnovo region during the late seventeenth century, centred on Arbanasi village.

One of those historians who thought the second Tarnovo uprising was legend not history was Halim's tutor at Anadolu University, Dr Sadik. Halim, however, was convinced that the events of the second uprising were authentic and often argued this point with his tutor. Dr Sadik for his part could never understand why this was so important to his earnest young student and sometimes Halim did not understand this either. In any event he was excited to find that Tim and Margot, the host family, lived in the very village of Arbanasi. Immediately he sent his own details to Tim and waited eagerly for a reply.

Only a couple of hours later Tim visited the site to see if anyone had expressed an interest in his listing.

"You only added our name yesterday," said Margot. "Nobody would have even seen it yet let alone made up their mind to apply."

Tim brushed off Margot's comments and persisted with his search. Five minutes later he was goading Margot for her negativity.

"O, ye of little faith, we already have our first potential worker. How wrong can someone be?"

"Before you get excited check whether he's a naturist and has clicked on the wrong host family," retorted Margot.

"I'll ignore that comment," said Tim, rather pompous now. "His name is Halim. He's a young Turkish lad just finished at university studying history. Apparently some rebellion against the Ottoman Empire took place here and he has studied the period. That is one of the reasons he wants to come."

"So it's not because of the crap you wrote about the work we want doing?" asked Margot with undisguised cynicism.

"I am sure it helped." said Tim taking the loftier position and refusing to exchange blows with Margot who seemed hell bent on irritating him.

Eventually she gave up and was herself curious to read about the young man who could well be living with them in a few weeks' time. She read his post over Tim's shoulder.

"He sounds very eager," she commented.

"Yes and he also sounds very nice," said Tim.

"Yes he does," Margot conceded. "And he looks nice too."

Still standing behind him Margot put her arms gently around Tim's neck as a sign of a truce between them. She suggested that they write back to invite the young man to join them.

"Maybe we should say for a month at first if that suits him and review it as we go on," she added.

"Good idea," Tim agreed. "I'll write back now," said Tim remaining business-like.

"No, I'll do it," said Margot emphatically.

With a smile of satisfaction that he ensured was not seen by Margot, Tim left her to it.

A few days later Tim and Vladimir were sitting in the village bar exchanging news. Tim often reflected on the differences between Britain and Bulgaria that he now so easily took for granted. On this occasion he smiled to himself regarding the ease with which he now thought of their current setting as a 'village bar'. It was in fact simply a shop with two metal-framed tables outside and a bench and six odd chairs as seating. The choice of drinks was restricted to bottled beer, one type of red wine or homemade rakia. All three beverages were served in a plastic cup so thin you could hardly hold it without squashing the cup and spilling the drink. The beer was from the same fridge as housed the cheese and ham for the shop. Except in exceedingly warm weather the fridge was switched off as an economy measure. In all his time in Bulgaria this was the only thing that Tim had ever complained about. Now each time he approached the bar he could hear the fridge whirr into action.

Vladimir was looking glum and soon Tim discovered why. When he heard about the blind removal man he could not stop laughing at his neighbour's misfortune.

"And just for good measure he is to live with you as well?" he said between further bouts of laughter.

Vladimir conceded that this was indeed the case.

"I had no idea that Bulgarians were so committed to equal opportunities. You are even employing a support worker for him. It's marvellous."

Tim burst into laughter again. Vladimir had no idea what equal opportunities meant, but he was damn sure he wasn't committed to it at all.

"What can I do? My mother and her sister have tricked me into this. They are like two witches."

"And what about the young sister, your other cousin? Is she the third member of the coven?" Tim asked.

"Good God, no. She is more like an angel than a witch. She is beautiful, Tim. You won't believe it when you see her," said Vladimir.

"I'll look forward to it," said Tim with conviction.

"She poses another problem entirely," said Vladimir. "If she starts wandering around the house in her bra and pants I won't be able to bear it."

"But she's your cousin, Vladimir. You must remember that."

"You think I don't know that?" said Vladimir, his concern rising as he spoke. "Believe me, it does not make it any easier."

Feeling his neighbour's anxiety, but also thinking he had probably taken the mickey enough now, Tim decided to change the subject.

"As it happens I've got some news of my own," he ventured his eyes twinkling.

"Well I hope it's better than mine," said Vladimir solemnly.

"Yes, I think it is really good news. We have a young man coming to live with us and work for us too." Tim could not resist putting the boot in, although his friend was already down. "The difference is we don't have to pay him!" and after a pause he added "Oh yes, and of course he can see."

Tim started to chuckle and soon he was rolling with laughter again, holding his sides. Vladimir had never understood British humour and in particular he failed to understand why they especially liked to laugh at their friends' expense. It was a very strange way to behave, he thought indignantly, but Tim's laughter showed no sign of abating.

"I am sorry, Vlado, but even you must be able to see the funny side of it," said Tim.

Vladimir decidedly could not.

Chapter Five

Momchil had been born with very little sight and by the time he was ten years old he was completely blind. His little sister, Denitsa, had been his eyes since then and the pair had become inseparable. Except for a few odd jobs for neighbours in his village, he had never worked and now at twenty four he at last had a real opportunity thanks to the kindness of his cousin. Momchil did not know Vladimir well, but as his mother had said blood is thicker than water. Nevertheless, his cousin must be an exceptional man to be prepared to take him on. Momchil was determined not to let his cousin down, but he was understandably nervous that he would not be able to cope.

Denitsa, God bless her, would hear none of it when he expressed his doubts to her.

"Of course you will be able to cope, Momchil. You are big and strong. You could probably lift a wardrobe or a dining table on your own, let alone together with our cousin. You will be fine."

"But I can't see!" he exclaimed. "How can I lift what I cannot see?"

"If I can see it then you can see it, just as it has always been. Now have you got your bag packed? Uncle Nedyalko will be here soon to take us to Arbanasi. I am so excited and so should you be."

Momchil confirmed that his bag was ready. As usual his wonderful sister was irrepressible. If she believed he would be alright then he would. He smiled at her and instantly felt her arms around his neck in a comforting embrace.

"I am excited too," he said.

Uncle Nedyalko had bought his Trabant motor car from an East German in 1990. Günther, as he was known, had gone to West Germany from Saxony after the fall of the Berlin Wall, but did not like it there. He had ended up in Bulgaria where he said that he felt more comfortable. He had arrived in Nedyalko's village almost penniless and the only saleable commodity he owned was his Trabant. The car was already ten years old when Nedyalko bought it and he had driven a very hard bargain. The old car had served him well and was still going strong. Günther had died two years earlier still complaining that Nedyalko had swindled him. Uncle Nedyalko was glad to have him off his back.

When the Trabant arrived outside their home Uncle Nedyalko gave a beep of the horn to let Momchil and Denitsa know that he was there. It was unnecessary as they had heard the car coming from two streets away. In East Germany the Trabants had been advertised as having room for four adults and luggage. Unfortunately, Nedyalko had done some modifications to his car that included removing the front passenger seat which he now used as a garden chair. Getting Momchil and all their luggage into the vehicle was therefore something of a challenge given that Momchil was six feet tall and weighed approximately fifteen stone. Thankfully his sister was very small and slim and weighed no more than eight stone. Consequently brother and sister looked quite comical squashed together on the back seat with a pile of luggage on top of them. Once loaded the old car roared off in the direction of Arbanasi.

*

Halim had arrived in Sofia by train and was now completing the last part of his journey, travelling from Sofia to Veliko Tarnovo by bus. The bus was surprisingly modern and comfortable which was just as well as the trip took three hours. He was glad to see the sign welcoming people to the old city indicating that his journey was at last coming to an end. Halim alighted from the bus and looked across at the beautiful, but rather ramshackle renaissance buildings of the old town set along a tangle of cobbled lanes high above the dramatic bends of the Yantra River. It was an impressive sight. Tim had told him to ring when he arrived at the bus station in Veliko Tarnovo so that he could pick him up, but Halim had resolved to get a taxi to the village which he understood was only about fifteen minutes' drive. He wanted to make it plain from the start that he had no intention of being a nuisance to his kind hosts.

Halim had been warned that Bulgarian taxi drivers were prone to overcharging foreigners and he was determined not to let this happen to him. However, he struck lucky as the driver was himself Turkish and greeted his countryman warmly. The taxi driver wanted all the news from home and they were deep in conversation when Halim idly looking out of the window had the strangest of feelings.

"Where are we now?" he asked bewildered.

"We are just approaching Arbanasi. It is at the top of this hill," replied the taxi driver suddenly picking up on the tension in Halim's voice. "Is everything alright? It was Arbanasi you wanted, wasn't it?"

"Yes, yes, it is just that I seem to recognise everything," said Halim trying to order his thoughts.

They were approaching the village along a bumpy road surrounded by rocky countryside that seemed oddly familiar.

"That is nice that you are remembering things," said the driver encouragingly. "How long is it since you were here?"

"That's just it," Halim replied. "I have never been here before in my life."

There were only three English families in the village and the driver had given rides to all of them so when Halim said Tim's name the driver was able to drop him outside. Halim looked across at the house and at once his eyes played tricks on him. For a second he found himself staring at a completely different house, considerably older and more humble. Beside the house was a huge oak tree giving shade to the front porch. This house aroused in him a feeling of longing mixed with sadness. The feeling was so strong he felt himself going faint. The taxi driver's voice seemed to be coming from a different time or place, but eventually he found himself back in the taxi with the cabby asking anxiously if he was alright. Halim was flustered and confused, but tried to get a grip of himself.

"I am sorry. I don't know what came over me. I guess it has been a long trip."

The driver was now starting to feel a little alarmed himself and when Halim took his bags and paid the fare he was quite glad to get away, the novelty of meeting a fellow countryman having long since deserted him.

The vision of the older house had thankfully faded away and as a historian Halim could place the house he now saw before him as having been built in the first half of the nineteenth century towards the end of the period of Ottoman rule. This he knew from his studies was referred to as the period of Bulgarian National Revival, or 'Renaissance'. The house had been sympathetically renovated, he thought, the only departure from the original design being the roof. This would originally have been made from huge stone slabs, but was now constructed using modern tiles. Nevertheless it was a fine house. Alongside it stood the same oak tree that he had seen in his vision. Eventually he recovered his equilibrium and Halim approached the door which opened just as he was about to knock.

"Hi, you must be Halim. We were just beginning to think the bus had been delayed and here you are. You should have rung. Tim would have…"

Suddenly Margot remembered her manners.

"Listen to me wittering on! I am Margot, how do you do?"

Halim was on safer ground now. This is how he had imagined it with a nice English couple asking 'How do you do?' A friendly looking man with a beaming smile suddenly appeared behind Margot.

"And I'm Tim." he announced.

"I am very pleased to meet you both," Halim replied rather formally. "I am indeed Halim."

Soon the three of them were seated in the living room with a cup of tea and a plate of Swiss roll. It was the only cake in the shops that Margot recognised. The furnishings in the living room were a mixture of British and Bulgarian. Tim and Margot had brought very little with them from home other than table lamps, pictures and other small items, having decided that the cost of transporting their large pieces of furniture was prohibitive. Also a lot of their furniture had been part of their lives for a long time and Margot wanted to make a fresh start in a new home and a new country. The floor had been laid with a reasonably expensive laminate which was partially covered with two traditional Bulgarian handwoven woollen rugs. There was a huge wood burning stove in one corner of the room and two very plain two-seater sofas. A glass top coffee table and two small occasional tables with table lamps completed the fairly simple décor. Margot and Halim sat opposite each other on the two sofas while Tim perched precariously on the arm of Margot's sofa wondering how in the coming days he would get across to Halim that he was in his seat.

Halim was telling the English couple about himself, but up to now he had said nothing to them about the weird familiarity he felt in Arbanasi, at least not until Tim asked a routine question.

"I remember that you said you had studied the history of this area. Have you ever been here before?"

Halim hesitated, but quickly decided it would be dishonest not to share what he had felt since arriving here. Anyway it was causing him some concern and he thought he would benefit from telling someone.

"No, I have never been here before, but everything I see somehow seems familiar."

Unlike Tim, Margot immediately noticed the oddness and anxiety in his voice, but chose to ignore it for the time being at least.

"I suppose if you have studied things that have happened in this area you are bound to feel you know the place even when you have never been here before," said Margot trying to put the young man at his ease. "You must have put your heart and soul into your work," she added with a smile.

It was true that Halim had studied the events that took place here with a passion, a passion that he had never really understood and what had happened since his arrival only added to the mystery.

"I am sure you are correct, Mrs Margot, that will be the reason."

Margot laughed inwardly. "Just plain Margot will be fine," she said and at that grabbed his bag. "Come on, I'll show you your room." And with Halim following obediently she headed for the stairs leading to the lower floor.

*

Just a month ago Vladimir had been perfectly happy. He enjoyed being in Arbanasi, an attractive and interesting village where he had lived all his life and where he had many friends. He also enjoyed his own company and was content living alone. Just to add variety to daily life he had an English couple living next door with whom he got on well. Tim in particular had become a good friend and it was thanks to him that Vladimir now had a successful business. Why could he not have left it at that? With a degree of self-rebuke Vladimir admitted to himself that he had wanted to play the big shot and have staff that he could order about instead of running the business on his own. Tim had warned him that he should wait until the van business was properly thriving before considering employing someone, but he had not listened. Now he had lumbered himself with two totally unsuitable employees and would be lucky if he could get the equivalent of one person's work out of the two of them put together. On top of that they were coming to live with him and he knew that his mother would be on his case to ensure he looked after his two cousins properly. Passing a mirror Vladimir saw a reflection of himself. A once good looking young man he was now an idiot in early middle age still capable of being duped by his mother. He gave his reflection a mock punch under the chin.

"Vladimir, you are nothing but a fool."

He could hear Uncle Nedyalko's Trabant pulling up outside with a cough and a final sigh as his uncle switched off the absurdly loud motor. Vladimir's humiliation was going to be witnessed by his old uncle who no doubt would be giving his two sisters, Vladimir's mother and aunt, a detailed report of how they had all been received. The whole thing was a dreadful conspiracy. Still, this was how it was so he might as well make the best of it. Vladimir would receive his cousins and uncle with the proper hospitality as befitted close family. With this in mind he went to open the door to greet them as soon as they were out of the car. Uncle Nedyalko was already on the pavement and was easing Momchil out of the back seat. As Vladimir approached Denitsa got out from the other side of the old vehicle and looked up to greet her cousin with a smile.

"Vladimir, how are you? It is a pleasure to see you again."

Vladimir stared at the girl who even in old jeans and a sweat shirt looked utterly divine. He was only half aware that his mouth was hanging open.

"For God's sake put your tongue away, man, and come and help your cousin out of the car," commanded his uncle.

Trying to ignore the embarrassment caused by Nedyalko's caustic remark, Vladimir sprang into action and virtually yanked Momchil onto the pavement.

"You are all very welcome," exclaimed Vladimir trying desperately to avert his eyes from his young cousin. "Most welcome!" he repeated.

"Yes, yes, more to the point have you got any rakia in the house? I am parched," his uncle replied and with that he left Vladimir to take charge of his guests. Letting himself in he went in search of the bottle without waiting for an invitation. As far as he was concerned his mission was complete.

At the car Denitsa quickly took charge of her brother. Vladimir, as is the way with people who have no experience of disability, stood there desperately wanting to help, but with no clue as to how. Once he had found his feet and his dignity had been restored Momchil offered his hand which Vladimir shook warmly and seemed unsure as to when, if at all, he should let go. Denitsa suppressed a giggle.

"Don't worry, cousin. With a little help, Momchil can manage anything."

At this, Momchil's chest puffed out with pride, and he decided that the time for his prepared thank you speech had arrived. However, he was only a few words into it when his little sister cut him off.

"Not now, Momchil. Let's get inside and sat down and then we can all get to know each other better. We'll have to hurry otherwise Vladimir will have no rakia left."

Although slightly deflated Momchil as always did as his sister suggested and taking her arm firmly, allowed himself to be led inside.

*

Halim sat on a smart leather armchair in the small converted bedroom. Noticing the bars on the window, so common in houses from this period, he smiled to himself to think that they had been erected to keep marauding Turks out of the house and now here he was a Turkish guest in the barred room. He was glad to be here after a long and rather arduous journey and his hosts were obviously lovely people, but despite all that he was still very unsettled. The feeling that he had been in this village before remained with him and continued to bother him. Now he was inside he was at least certain that he had not been in the house before. However, the feelings he had experienced when he first arrived in the taxi and, in particular, the vision of the old house sat next to the ancient oak tree that he could now partly see out of his small window were disturbing indeed.

Halim thought back to the things he knew about Arbanasi from his studies at university. The village had a rich history based mainly around the holy places, monasteries and cloisters, which were such a feature of Arbanasi and had made the place a favourite destination for tourists. Oddly though his interest whilst at college had focused on the second Tarnovo uprising of sixteen eighty six which was said to have started in Arbanasi. This interest had developed despite the fact that there was only very sketchy historical information about these events. Why had this always so fascinated him? His tutor, Dr Sadik, always found it curious and he was now thinking the same. Perhaps now that he was here he would find something that linked him to the place, although he could not for the life of him think what that may be. Perhaps the house he had imagined would be a clue. The low and humble building certainly pre-dated the Renaissance period. As soon as he had an opportunity he would visit the museum in Veliko Tarnovo and see if he could find any impressions of the local architecture from the time of the second uprising. Halim stood up and looked out of the window to get a clearer view of the ancient oak. Was he being silly? Probably yes, but somehow he had to find some answers.

Back in the living room Tim and Margot were discussing their new lodger cum worker.

"He seems a nice enough lad," said Margot, "Although I don't quite know what to make of his saying everything seems so familiar. What does he mean?"

"It was just a harmless remark. I think he just meant he was feeling at home," suggested Tim.

"You are an idiot if you think that, Tim. That is definitely not what he was meaning. Didn't you notice how agitated he was over it?" replied Margot impatiently. "I think he had some sort of Déjà vu experience. I think it had really unsettled him."

"I reckon you are going a bit over the top there, Margot. He was probably just tired from the journey," Tim retorted.

"Just stick to diggers and trucks and leave the psychology to me," said Margot smiling. "Well, he's certainly an extremely nice looking young man," she added. "I am sure we can agree on that at least. He will be causing a stir amongst the local girls, that I can assure you."

"I am sure he would if there were any young women in Arbanasi. I think you are probably the youngest woman living here!" said Tim, then adding unwisely, "Much as I love you, Margot, I don't think you could be classed as a young woman."

"You be careful, old man. You might just live to regret that remark," she countered.

Tim poked his tongue out at her playfully and there the conversation ended because they could both hear Halim's footsteps on the stairs.

*

That night Denitsa lay awake and recalled the events of the day with considerable pleasure. Predictably, Uncle Nedyalko had drunk too much rakia and she could hear his gentle snores coming from the next room. As usual though he drank his way through the majority of Vladimir's only bottle without offending anyone. Her dear cousin had wanted to go to the local shop and buy him another bottle, but through a series of gestures that her uncle had not noticed Denitsa indicated to Vladimir that this was not a good idea. Within ten minutes she was fully vindicated as Uncle Nedyalko fell into a deep contented sleep on the old horsehair sofa.

In just one short evening Denitsa had become really fond of her cousin Vladimir. He just could not do enough to make them all feel welcome and she was genuinely amazed to discover what an excellent cook he was. She had not expected any more than some bread and tomatoes on arrival, but instead they were treated to a three course meal. The main course of spinach balls in white sauce with sauté potatoes was absolutely delicious and her brother Momchil had been overwhelmed by the hospitality. Denitsa did not think that she had ever seen Momchil so happy and this particularly endeared her to Vladimir because it was his kindness that had brought this about. At the second attempt Momchil had made his prepared thank you speech and Vladimir seemed quite moved by it. Her brother could be so sweet and she prayed that once the serious business of working with their cousin started it would all work out for him. At least she no longer had to worry that it would just be her looking out for him. She could see that Vladimir would be anxious to help Momchil succeed. After all it was in everybody's interests to make this arrangement work.

Denitsa was aware that she was a pretty girl, but did not realise that most people would describe her as beautiful, exceptionally beautiful. She had dark almond shaped eyes under perfectly arched brows. Her high cheekbones and angular face were splendid examples of Balkan beauty. Her wide mouth was permanently on the verge of a smile. Denitsa smiled now as she recalled the look on her cousin's face when she got out of the car and laughed out loud as she remembered her uncle's disparaging remark about Vladimir needing to put his tongue away. They had all felt awkward for a moment and to hide his embarrassment Vladimir had immediately wanted to busy himself helping Momchil out of the car. She had hardly looked her best, but nevertheless it was nice to be admired by your elder cousin.

The lovely village of Arbanasi, was in complete contrast to the dull, grey village where she had been born and raised. Life here was going to be very pleasant, of that she was certain. Tomorrow was Sunday and her cousin had told her and Momchil that he never worked on the Sabbath so she would have a free day. Denitsa intended to use the time exploring her new home and the surrounding area. For once she would leave her brother behind. This day would be for her.

On Sunday morning she was up early, but not as early as Uncle Nedyalko who was already on his way home in the old Trabant. There was no sign of either Momchil or Vladimir so after a simple breakfast she wrote a cheerful note for her cousin and left the house. It was a glorious morning and Denitsa was in a mood that could only be described as joyful. She headed off out of the village anxious to see if the surrounding countryside was as lovely as the village itself. She had no particular route or direction in mind, but somehow her feet seemed to be walking with a purpose and soon she found herself on a path which she seemed to know. She did not and could not know this path she told herself, but suddenly there was no point pretending. Rounding a bend a well-tended field confronted her with rows of tomato and cucumber plants and beans growing up old canes made from twigs and branches collected in the woods nearby. Denitsa knew this field. Surely it was she that had planted these crops. She knew this to be so, but also knew that it could not be so. She tried, but could not fight off the absolute certainty that this field belonged to her and her family and that she had been coming here every day to plant and tend the crops.

"Good morning."

A young woman was approaching the field calling cheerily to her as she came. "I hope you weren't thinking of eating those tomatoes, 'cos they still be green," the girl said with humour. "If you want to pinch something you would be better going for the raspberries. They are just coming ripe now. Help yourself, why don't you?"

The girl who was a few years older than Denitsa had a mocking tone about her that intentionally left you unsure whether she was joking or not. The girl sensed Denitsa's uncertainty.

"Don't worry, I'm only messing. Take some raspberries, we've got plenty. They're delicious."

Denitsa reached for some raspberries feeling embarrassed but no longer unsure that the invitation was a genuine one.

"Thank you," she said. "Gosh, they are nice."

The girl had the same dark hair as Denitsa herself and similar Balkan features. She was however fuller of figure and somehow sturdier on her feet. But it was not so much her appearance that seemed familiar as her manner.

"Where are you from?" the girl asked her. "I don't remember seeing you before."

Where was she from? Suddenly Denitsa did not know how to answer, but decided on sticking to the facts she was certain of.

"I have come to live and work with my cousin, Vladimir," she replied. "My brother and I arrived yesterday."

"Oh, I heard you were coming. He is a lovely man. Just you mind he keeps his hands off you. He's been telling everyone what a beauty you are. Holds a candle for you I reckon."

Denitsa feigned outrage, pointing out that they were first cousins, but secretly she was pleased that Vladimir had been talking about her in this way. However, nothing got past this jovial girl.

"You needn't pretend to me. I can see you like the look of him too," she teased. "He is a good looker, mind."

Simultaneously, the faces of the two girls broke into wide smiles and Denitsa could feel her red flush subsiding again. Denitsa had found a friend and sooner or later, but not now, she would tell her about the connection she felt to the field. Having just met the girl, who finally introduced herself as Galena, she did not want her to think that she was going out of her mind.

*

Vladimir walked into his kitchen and noticed for the first time that the place was looking worn and grubby. He noticed it now because suddenly it mattered. He was aware that he now had a young woman using the same space and was conscious that she would notice things that up until now he had not noticed. In short, the whole house, not just the kitchen, looked tired, typical of a place inhabited by a single bloke with no woman in his life. He made himself a promise to spruce the place up a bit.

Amongst the general clutter on the kitchen table he noticed a piece of paper neatly folded with his name on the front. Correctly assuming it to be from Denitsa he picked it up and immediately felt disappointed when he read his cousin's note and realised that she would be missing most of the day. He had hoped to show her and Momchil around the village and even take them to see Veliko Tarnovo, in his opinion the most enchanting city in Bulgaria. Having no experience of people with disabilities he had briefly wondered about how to show Momchil a city that he cannot actually see. He was conscious not to exclude him from anything and had decided that he would make all the same offers of hospitality to the two of them and leave Denitsa to ensure that Momchil got as much from the experience as possible. She seemed confident and competent in this role which she carried out in a completely matter of fact way, mixed with admirable grace. In fact there was altogether a great deal to admire about Denitsa and again he found himself regretting her absence.

Having been forced by his young cousin's absence to abandon his plans for the day Vladimir began to consider how in a practical sense he would manage a day on his own with Momchil. Just as he was considering this his anxiety was heightened by the sound of Momchil shuffling towards the kitchen.

"Good morning, Cousin Vladimir," Momchil boomed. "Looks like just us boys this morning. Denitsa went out early and Uncle Nedyalko earlier still in his old Trabant. God, the noise that car makes just starting up I am surprised it still has the power to go anywhere!"

Vladimir suddenly realised that he had not given his old uncle a second thought until that moment and had no idea that he had already left.

"It is a bit of an old banger," Vladimir agreed. "Still, it seems to get him about."

Rubbing his stomach Momchil abruptly changed the subject. "Lovely dinner last night. I can't believe I feel hungry again. Must be the country air."

Vladimir jumped into action. "Yes, of course. I'll get some breakfast together. Come and sit down."

He clumsily latched on to Momchil's elbow and in his eagerness to help him to a chair, himself tripped over a small stool and went crashing to the ground. Momchil at first looked concerned, but when he heard Vladimir stumbling to his feet concern turned to mirth and in spite of his fear that it could be deemed impolite he could not stop a full blooded guffaw ripping through him.

"I guess I'm not very good at this," said Vladimir showing a mastery of the power of understatement.

As he got to his feet he put his arm round his cousin and lustily laughed along with him.

"We'll have breakfast," said Vladimir finally regaining control of himself, "And then we'll go next door and you can meet our English neighbours, Tim and Margot. Do you speak English, Momchil?"

"Jawohl!" came the not altogether encouraging reply.

Vladimir allowed himself a smile and set about preparing breakfast. This removal business is certainly going to be interesting, he thought to himself.

Having said her goodbyes to Galena, Denitsa reluctantly left the field and was soon on the road again leading back towards the village. She was deep in thought, trying to make sense of the last hour, but it simply did not make any sense. She had heard of a phenomenon known as a déjà vu, but had never experienced it. Perhaps this was what had happened to her, although the intensity of the experience had quite unsettled her. Denitsa was certainly not ready to return to the village just at that moment where Momchil would no doubt be waiting for her. She needed more time on her own to try and get her equilibrium back. Coming round the corner she saw a signpost to Veliko Tarnovo and without a second thought she took the turning to the city just five kilometres away.

Soon she was heading down a steep hill and after a short while she could see the city below her. Denitsa had been told that Veliko Tarnovo was an exceptional place, but she had not anticipated such a lovely sight. From her position above the city she could take in the whole place in one glance. To the left she could see the famous fortress of Tsarevets with the River Yantra meandering around it before flowing on to dissect the old city. The red roofed houses seemed to be on the verge of falling into the river, but had in fact remained on their perch above the Yantra for several hundred years. She hurried on eager to walk the famous streets and take in the atmosphere of the old part of town that she had heard so much about.

Denitsa walked on two or three hundred metres, all the time retaining an excellent view of the city beneath her. Slowly she became aware of a rumbling sound that seemed to get louder as she listened. The source of the noise appeared to lie some way ahead of her and she instinctively increased her pace. The rumbling became more distinct and Denitsa was sure she could hear loud voices amongst the general tumult and commotion. Suddenly she found herself looking at a rocky outcrop beside the road and the second her eyes fell upon it the noise stopped abruptly. She stared at the outcrop, convinced that this had been the source of the sounds she had heard as she approached. Without warning Denitsa became suddenly dizzy and as she tottered and fell she saw through half closed eyes a shadowy image of a young man on the ground with a sword through his heart. The last thing she remembered of the vision as she was passing out was that she, Denitsa, was looking over him sobbing.

"Are you alright, young lady?"

An old gentleman had the palm of his hand under Denitsa's head and was trying to raise her gently into a sitting position. As she slowly came to his kind old eyes were looking at her with concern. When he saw she was waking up he allowed himself a gentle smile.

"It'll be the heat I reckon. You should have worn a hat in this weather."

He admonished her gently and then produced a small bottle of mineral water that Denitsa thoughtlessly drained.

"Thank you. That feels better. Where am I?" asked Denitsa. "Gosh, I am sorry. I seem to have drank all of your water. How selfish of me," she added.

"Don't worry I have more," the old man replied, but to Denitsa's disappointment he did not produce it.

She still felt as if she could drink another ten bottles.

"Where is this place? I don't remember how I got here," said Denitsa repeating her earlier question.

"You are on the road from Veliko Tarnovo to Arbanasi. You are not from round here, then?" the old man enquired.

"No, but I moved to Arbanasi yesterday, to my cousin's house. I was just having a look round. But where is this place? I heard things; loud rumbling noises; men shouting above the din."

The old man looked around as if he needed to reacquaint himself with a place that had become over familiar to him. He searched his memory banks before answering slowly.

"Well there is nothing particular about this part of the road, not these days anyway. Mind you, the rocky area just across the way is supposed to be the scene of some battle or other around the seventeenth century. Something to do with an uprising against the Turks, I think."

Denitsa stared at him, open mouthed.

"That's it! That's what I heard. I heard the battle raging then I passed out."

She hesitated and then to the old man's amazement she made an unlikely claim.

"I was there. I was at the scene of the battle. I was there. There was a dead man. I, I think I killed him!"

At this the old man's amazement turned to alarm. "Now, don't be taking on so. You've got heat stroke." The old man proved as good as his word and produced another bottle of water.

Denitsa drank the water greedily in the hope that it would restore some sense to her. Again she drained the bottle, but this time did not apologise. Her fevered mind, for so she believed it to be, was working overtime, exhausting her. Now her words became barely audible.

"I was here at the battle," she insisted. "I know I was."

The old man decided that action would speak louder than words. The young lady was obviously delirious and had to be got out of the sun and taken home as soon as possible.

"Who is your cousin?" he asked.

"Vladimir, Vladimir Pavlov." Denitsa's answer was mechanical like a lost child telling a police officer where she lived.

"I know him," said the old man with relief. "I will drive you home."

He helped Denitsa to her feet and led her to his car. She noted absently that the car was more abandoned than parked. No doubt the man had stopped suddenly on seeing her lying by the road. Although the old gentleman opened the door to the front passenger seat, she climbed into the back of the car trying to create some distance between the reality of the moment and her crowded thoughts. The old man too was quite grateful for the silence created by the distance between them. The beautiful young girl's remarks had started to alarm him and as he approached Vladimir's house he felt quite relieved that his 'good deed' was coming to an end. Suddenly he was jolted out of this sense of relief as Denitsa let out a loud gasp from behind him. She was staring, not at Vladimir's house, but at that of Margot and Tim next door. Her eyes were fixed on the ancient oak tree and she was making even less sense than before.

*

The advantage of rising early was that Uncle Nedyalko arrived back in his home village at around breakfast time. He was hungry too. Rather than go home where only some two day old bread and a few tomatoes awaited him, he decided to head to his sister Rada's house. Her deceased husband had always insisted on a good breakfast and although she had always complained about this ritual she had continued to start the day in this fashion even after his death. There was every prospect that, if his timing was right, he could look forward to some fresh homemade rolls with egg, cheese and sausage.

His sister's house was set far back from the road, partially obscured by three towering pine trees. It was a plain house finished in white plaster with a brown tiled roof. Several tiles were missing. It had once been a vibrant house with a young family. Now his brother in law had passed away and equally significant for Rada was the loss of her son and daughter who Nedyalko had just deposited in Arbanasi. From now on life would be very different in the old place. Nedyalko stepped onto the veranda. The boards were thin and cracked, frozen by decades of winters, and baked by as many summers.

"Come in, come in, Nedyalko. You are just in time for breakfast."

The old man's eyes sparkled. "I'm not sure, Rada, I am more tired than hungry. It is a long drive in the old car. Perhaps just a roll."

"Don't be ridiculous," his sister retorted. "A man needs a good breakfast. My Nikolai, God rest his soul, swore by it. Now come and sit down and tell me all about Momchil's and Denitsa's arrival at their cousin's house. Had he prepared some food for them, at least?"

With mock reluctance, that did not for a moment fool his sister, Nedyalko sat down at Rada's breakfast table laden with food. He looked around longingly as Rada poured the coffee.

"Come on, man, speak up! I want to know everything," she continued.

"Well, I hardly know where to start," replied Nedyalko.

"What do you mean, you don't know where to start?" asked his sister impatiently.

"I mean shall I have egg first or sausage?" he replied with a glint in his eye.

Rada was used to her brother's little jokes. She had fallen victim to them all her life.

"If you do not answer my questions properly you won't get egg, sausage or anything else," Rada replied firmly.

"Yes, the egg to start, I think. If I start with spicy sausage I won't taste anything after that."

Rada waited, not altogether patiently, for her brother to spin out his silly game.

"Yes, well, the arrival in Arbanasi of your two dear children," he continued at last. "I would watch that nephew of yours if I were you, Rada. He took a real shine to your Denitsa. He couldn't keep his eyes off her."

As her brother had intended Rada was momentarily distracted and she started a tirade against the way all the men in the village ogle her daughter and that she thought that she could at least trust Denitsa's cousin to look after her honour. Nedyalko realised that he had gone too far and anyway he had eaten his egg and his sausage was loaded on the plate ready.

"No, no, don't worry. Vladimir is a good boy. Of course he found her attractive, any man would, but he will look after her just as you would expect from an elder cousin. He was a real gentleman yesterday."

"Then why did you try to send my blood pressure through the roof? I have a blind boy and a beautiful daughter both of whom I worry about miles from their mother's care and all you can do is make fun of me!"

With this Rada burst into tears and, as was intended, her brother felt awful. Nedyalko apologised and immediately fell into line. He told the whole story of their arrival, including the wonderful, friendly reception by Vladimir and the excellent dinner he had cooked. Prompted by Rada, he gave the fullest information about the meal right down to the details of the salad dressing. The only detail he omitted was his own consumption of three quarters of a bottle of rakia. In any event there was no need to provide this piece of information as his sister would have guessed this already. With Rada's fears allayed peace reigned and Nedyalko settled down to enjoy the rest of his excellent breakfast.

*

Over in Arbanasi Vladimir and Momchil had also eaten a good breakfast and when they called next door Tim was sitting in the garden with Halim telling him about themselves and their new life in Bulgaria. So far, Halim had been given no information about his work duties and Tim was showing no sign of telling him anything. However, it was Sunday so he could maybe expect to be told something tomorrow. Already his main concern was when he would find time to visit the museum in Veliko Tarnovo. On the other hand, Tim seemed to be extremely easy going and would definitely allow him time to do this, possibly even offer to accompany him.

"Good morning, Tim. This is my cousin, Momchil," Vladimir called out heartily.

He had already learned enough not to introduce Momchil as his *blind* cousin. Tim got up and walked over. He took hold of Momchil's hand and shook it warmly.

"You are very welcome, Momchil. I hope you will like it in Arbanasi."

"So far I like it very much," Momchil replied politely, but indeed truthfully.

Remembering his manners, Tim turned back towards Halim who had already got to his feet and was following behind.

"We also have a new member of the household," said Tim and after formal introductions the four men sat down to get acquainted.

"Four coffees, is it?" asked Margot as she too appeared outside.

Vladimir, Momchil and Halim all stood to receive her while Tim remained seated a little displaced by the show of politeness towards his wife. The introductions were repeated and Margot without stopping beyond saying hello turned back towards the kitchen to fetch some drinks. Three coffees with no milk and two sugars was easy to remember. She knew that even so early Tim would probably prefer beer, but he would have to make do with milky coffee, at least until she had established whether Halim was a strict Moslem. Even if he was she would not expect Tim to stop drinking in his own house, but allowing him his first beer at ten in the morning would not give the best of impressions.

"So where is your beautiful sister that I have heard so much about?" Tim enquired of Momchil.

Vladimir looked a little uncomfortable remembering his remarks to Tim about his fear of her wandering around in her bra and panties. In his experience you could never judge what an Englishman may repeat. After all their primary source of humour was usually at the expense of a friend. Just then, however, Margot reappeared and Vladimir knew that now at least Tim would remain reasonably discreet. Momchil informed the group that his sister had gone out early to explore and they were not sure when she would be back. Vladimir gave a smile of affirmation.

Denitsa climbed out of the old gentleman's car and stood on the roadside staring still at the old oak tree. Without her particularly noticing, the old chap had also got out of his car, apparently intending to deliver her to her cousin.

"Come on, I'll take you in and explain what has happened."

Suddenly Denitsa became aware of the old man standing next to her. She definitely did not want her cousin, or her brother for that matter, to hear his account of what had taken place. It would only alarm them.

"No, no, you have been very kind. I am absolutely fine now. I will be OK, honestly. You have done more than enough. Thank you so much."

The old man was torn between what he regarded as his duty and his strong desire to get on his way.

"I really think I should at least take you to the door." The old man was half-heartedly insistent.

Denitsa looked at him with her beautiful dark almond shaped eyes. She put her hand on his arm and told him again that she was fine. The old man's determination melted away; he was unable to do other than what Denitsa wished.

"Take care of yourself, my dear," he found himself saying and obediently he got back into his car and drove away.

Almost at once Denitsa heard voices coming from the neighbours' garden and she quickly identified her brother's booming tones. If Momchil was there then so was Vladimir. Denitsa felt massive relief as she realised that their cousin's house was therefore empty. She walked quietly up the path and let herself in. At least she would have time to get her head straight. She went swiftly to her room and lay down on the bed. Without even trying her brain started listing the strange things that had occurred. Firstly there was her familiarity with the lane out of the village, followed immediately by the certainty, not only that she knew the field that the lane led to, but the impossible knowledge that her family owned it and that she had planted the crops! Then on the road to Veliko Tarnovo the sounds of a crowd, possibly even of a battle and the horrible vision of the young man lying dead on the ground and the belief that she was somehow responsible for his death. Finally there was the oak tree outside the house of Vladimir's neighbours. She was so familiar with this tree. None of this could be real and nothing that suggested itself could be true, but she knew, she knew absolutely, that it was all real and that the story unfolding was true. On top of everything else she believed that she was, or at least had been, part of that story.

Chapter Six

The following morning Tim and Margot got up early and after a coffee and some toast they sat down to make a list of things that Halim could help them with. After only a short while the list was already quite extensive and sensibly Margot called a halt to the exercise.

"If we make this list any longer, it will be really daunting for him, besides which he would have to work here for years!"

"Well he said he wanted to know exactly what we required of him so he will be glad to have a list," retorted Tim.

Margot was not convinced. "No, I think we should show him the list briefly so that he has an idea what sort of things he will be doing and then you can take some tasks from the list each day and ask Halim to do them. Of course if the jobs are difficult or need two people, as many of them do, you will need to work with him."

Tim knew this and had welcomed the arrival of Halim as a spur for him to get himself organised. Now however, with the sun already beating down the prospect of a daily routine of work did not seem so attractive. Margot was still in a practical frame of mind.

"The last thing is we must decide his working hours. How many hours is he supposed to work each day?"

"Anything up to eight hours a day," replied Tim, but realising that he was at the same time defining his own working day added, "But I thought five hours per day would be enough. I mean he is working for nothing."

Margot smiled to herself. Her husband was so transparent.

"Five hours a day will be fine," she agreed. "So what are you going to give him today?"

"I thought he could start by spreading the gravel that Vladimir brought on the drive. That is nice and straightforward," replied Tim.

"I thought you might say that as you won't have to help him," said Margot.

"I suppose that is true, although it never occurred to me," said Tim, feigning innocence. "Maybe I will help him for an hour until he gets the hang of it," he added magnanimously.

Shortly afterwards Halim appeared for breakfast at seven thirty, the time Margot had suggested and just before eight o clock he presented himself to Tim to be told his duties. Halim looked with interest at the list of jobs and did not seem at all fazed.

"That is very good. I will start right away. What do you want me to do first?"

Tim explained about the gravel.

"Yes, I saw it in the garden. That is no problem."

"I'll give you a hand for a bit and then leave you to it," said Tim and after twenty minutes, during which he ascertained that Halim worked more efficiently than he did and at double the speed, Tim was as good as his word and left him to it.

*

The following morning Denitsa woke up with a start as the events of yesterday raced around her brain. As she became properly awake she resolved to try and put the experiences of the previous day behind her, but for the time being that was proving impossible. Whatever else, the oak tree still stood in front of the house next door and still stirred in her feelings of familiarity that she could not explain. However, even if she could not get all that had happened out of her mind she must at least try and park these thoughts for another time if she could. For now at least she had to think about her brother. This was going to be a massive day for him.

Momchil too was acutely aware that this was the first morning of his new job alongside his cousin. They were due to leave the house in the van in about an hour's time and, although he would of course have the support of his sister Denitsa, Momchil was panic stricken. It was not just his awareness of his limitations that was causing him anxiety. This was the first day of his first ever proper job and he felt just as any sixteen year old might feel in the same position.

Momchil was stirred from his anxious thoughts by a crisp knock on his bedroom door. When the door was immediately opened making the inquiring knock completely superfluous he knew that it was his sister.

"What are you doing sitting here? Vladimir has made breakfast. Aren't you hungry?"

"Good morning, sister," he replied. "No, I am not really at all hungry, but if our kind cousin has made breakfast I will of course come and try and eat it."

Denitsa was having none of this nonsense. "What do you mean, try?" she said. "You have an appetite like a bear and I am famished. Come on he has put on a real spread."

Trying not to allow his sister to notice his sudden interest in the breakfast, Momchil took Denitsa's arm and followed her from the room.

Momchil was not the only one feeling nervous about the day ahead. Despite his reservations Vladimir had so far enjoyed having his genial cousin around the place and, since falling over himself the day before and them both having a good laugh about it, he was feeling more relaxed in handling Momchil's blindness. In addition, having the opportunity to spend time with his beautiful cousin, Denitsa, although somewhat unsettling, was a joy to him. Her sunny presence lit up the house like the first day of spring. However, today could either enhance or significantly mar the relationship building between the three cousins. Today they had to tackle the first job that had been passed to him by the huge furniture store on the outskirts of Veliko Tarnovo and if this was to become a long term source of work he dare not foul up. What the hell would they think when he turned up with a blind assistant? Well he would find out soon enough and if with Denitsa's assistance the job was done efficiently then surely it would not matter. After all, this was Bulgaria where almost anything passed as normal.

Throughout breakfast Denitsa chatted away in a manner that was guaranteed to banish any negative thoughts and soon both Momchil and Vladimir began to relax.

"I am so excited about today," she declared. "We are like the three Musketeers, nothing can stop us!"

"Except perhaps an eighteenth century iron bedstead weighing half a ton," replied Vladimir, rather drily.

"It may have defeated you before, cousin, but now you have Momchil. He has the strength of a lion."

Momchil smiled to himself. His sister was simply irrepressible.

Less than an hour later, Momchil, under the guiding eyes and commanding voice of his sister, was assisting his cousin in carrying a three seater sofa out of the furniture store and down the steps towards Vladimir's van. With the sofa safely deposited in the back of the van Vladimir held onto the side of the vehicle to catch his breath. Momchil on the other hand appeared unaffected by the exertion and stood by awaiting further instructions.

"What else are we getting from here?" he enquired.

Still breathing heavily Vladimir assured his cousin that was all for the time being. Their task now was just to deliver it.

"We have got to take it to an address in Gurko Street," he said. "It won't be easy to get the van down there. The road is so narrow," he added.

"Well, I am afraid I cannot help you there," Momchil replied. "I'm not sure it is a good idea for me to drive."

"I am not so sure about that," Vladimir asserted. "With Deni's help you could probably manage that as well."

The three cousins laughed and Denitsa gave both of them a big hug.

"What did I tell you?" she exclaimed. "All for one and one for all. Unstoppable!"

*

Halim had enjoyed his first day at work and already held his hosts, Tim and Margot, in high esteem. It was now three in the afternoon and Tim, who had some bits of business to conduct in Veliko Tarnovo himself, had given Halim a lift in. Tim had explained that the best way to get around the town was on foot and he had accordingly parked at the entrance to Gurko Street and given Halim directions to the museum. He had told him to walk the full length of Gurko Street until he came to the school and then to fork left up the path to the next level. Veliko Tarnovo was built on the side of a steep hill above the river Yantra and the various levels were reached via a series of old steps and steep paths. Tim had confidently informed him that as he reached the higher level he would see the museum on his right.

As he entered the historic Gurko Street he saw a plague on the wall explaining the origin of the street's name. The street was named after the Russian General Gurko who in 1877 had liberated the town from the yoke of Turkish Ottoman rule, a reminder to Halim that his country and Bulgaria had not always enjoyed cordial relations. As he walked along the picturesque cobbled street he could see a van about a hundred metres ahead that he recognised as the vehicle belonging to Tim's neighbour whom he had met the previous day. As he watched, Vladimir and Momchil came out of a nearby house and went to get into the van. Assisting Momchil into the passenger seat was a young woman whom he took to be Momchil's sister. He only caught a quick glimpse of her but even from a hundred metres away he could see how beautiful she was. As she disappeared into the truck and Vladimir drove away he felt a sense of disappointment. However, he reminded himself that, given she lived next door to him, he would have plenty of opportunities to get to know her. Such an effect did she have on him that for a moment Halim forgot what he was supposed to be looking out for until suddenly a large square school building came into view confirming he was on course.

Tim's directions turned out to be very accurate and soon Halim was standing in front of the museum. The museum was an impressive building set back and down from the road. It was of white stone with a tiled roof with ornate arched windows on both floors. Broad steps with a wrought iron balustrade led up to the entrance. In front of the building were three poplar trees, which enhanced rather than obscured the building, and a well-kept lawn on which quite a number of young children were playing. Most of the children were only five or six years old, but did not at first glance seem to be supervised. However, almost at once Halim noticed a small bar with green canopies a few steps away from the lawn. All the outside seats were occupied by watching mothers enjoying a drink and a chat while their kids played.

Halim walked up the steps and entered the museum with some trepidation equally unsure about what he was looking for and what he might discover. He was surprised to find that he could recall the image of the house he had seen in his mind's eye all too easily. As a historian and also given he was a newcomer to Bulgaria he found all the museum's exhibits fascinating and as a result his progress was constantly interrupted. However, eventually he found what he could be seeking, a display entitled 'Tarnovo Life through the Ages'.

The display started in the Middle Ages when Tarnovo had been the capital city of the Second Bulgarian Empire. This part of the display included an artist's impression of a nobleman's house, known as a Bolyar house, based on a ruin that had been excavated in Tarnovo in the late twentieth century. A photograph of the ruin was also on display. This made Halim hopeful that he would eventually find drawings of sixteenth and seventeenth century architecture as this is the period in which he believed the house his mind had conjured up would have stood.

As he read further he discovered that there were two types of common dwellings in the Middle Ages; semi-dug houses and over-ground houses. The latter were constructed in cities on levelled ground and usually had two stories. The semi-dug houses were more commonly built in villages and were dug in sloping terrain. The rear of the house was fully under the ground and the front was exposed. These houses were built of stones soldered with mud (in the parts over the ground) and the roof was made of timber. The depth of dug-in reached two meters and therefore the entrance door was from the exposed part. The floor was covered with bricks or plastered up with clay. A furnace was used for heating and the smoke came out from an opening on the roof. This description fitted the house of his imagination so accurately that Halim was starting to think his estimate of when the house had stood was wrong. However, as he continued to look at the display he was informed that these semi-dug houses continued to be used during the early and middle period of the Ottoman Empire.

Halim was fascinated, but for a moment his attention was taken by a presentation on worship showing local religious architecture through the ages, of particular interest to him because it included information about churches and monasteries from Arbanasi. His eyes fell on an artist's impression of a scene from the village in the seventeenth century showing the villagers of the time filing into church. And suddenly there it was! Nestled alongside the church was a small cluster of simple dwellings amongst which stood the house he had seen and next to it was the old oak tree.

Halim let out a gasp and reached behind him for a chair. He managed to sit down just as he became faint fearing for a moment that he was going to pass out. A young museum attendant, Petya Licheva, who had thus far been watching him more on account of his good looks than from any professional interest, rushed over.

"Are you alright?" she asked, slightly unsure of what to do, but Halim assured her there was nothing to worry about.

"It is nothing," he said. "I just felt a bit dizzy. It is passing now."

Not to be so easily put off the girl fetched a glass of water and handed it to him again seeking reassurance that nothing was amiss.

"It is really nothing," Halim told her. "It is just something I saw in the display. It took me by surprise. I will be fine."

The girl gave a nervous smile and Halim smiled back.

"I really am fine." he assured her.

The girl moved away reluctantly, turning as she did so to take a last look over her shoulder. She was rewarded with the discovery that the handsome young man was still smiling at her.

Shortly afterwards Halim stood up and made to leave. Petya noticed at once and checked the time on her phone. There were still ten minutes to go to the end of her shift. Looking around she could not see the museum's fussy little curator lurking nearby and quickly made a decision. She would take a chance and leave early. She gave her friend and colleague, Desi, a strangled smile and grabbed her coat.

"See you tomorrow," she said in a barely audible voice.

Desi had never seen her friend in such a hurry. It was so out of character. On the verge of asking her what was up, Desi followed her friend's eyes to the young man leaving the building. She smiled to herself. There was no need to ask.

Trying not to be too obvious, Petya quickly caught up with Halim who still seemed lost in his own thoughts. In an attempt not to appear too brazen, Petya remained in her role as the concerned museum assistant.

"You still seem very preoccupied," she ventured. "Are you sure you are alright?"

Halim looked up surprised. Until she spoke he had not realised she was alongside him. He smiled to himself. The young woman was quite lovely and was no doubt more accustomed to being chased by men rather than vice-versa.

"It was a picture I saw in the museum, just a drawing in fact. It sort of unsettled me," he replied politely.

"What picture was it? I probably know it. My colleague Desi and I set up most of that display, but I can't think of anything that would spook someone."

Petya was looking at him carefully, unintentionally disarming him. Halim thought a moment before answering her.

"I would tell you, but it does not make any sense. You would think me odd, even slightly deranged."

"I somehow doubt that." She was smiling now. "You look pretty sane to me. Tell me about it."

Halim was starting to find the idea of telling this girl all about what he had seen and felt since arriving in Arbanasi quite irresistible. She seemed genuinely interested.

"I'll tell you what," he said suddenly. "I passed a nice hotel cum restaurant just along here. Let me buy you a coffee."

"That would be lovely," she replied.

Less than fifteen minutes later Halim and Petya arrived at the Gurko Hotel. For the first time Halim noticed how big the hotel was and was doubtful that there would be enough outside visitors to fill the place on a regular basis. However, it was clear that the hotel was thriving. From the outside the establishment was enchanting, the traditional revivalist architecture enhanced by the best display of plants and hanging baskets he had ever seen. Once inside, sitting in the traditional Balkan surroundings of the hotel, Halim was inclined to tell his lovely companion the whole story. Nevertheless he was still uncertain how she would react. After all, he did not know anything about her. She had been kind to him in the museum and she had a natural warmth that was reassuring, but his tale was a strange one and she might think he was crazy or, even worse, just laugh at him.

Suddenly Halim realised that her opinion mattered to him. He was still hesitant, but gently she was pressing him to open up. He had after all virtually invited her here for coffee on that understanding. Once he started to speak everything came flooding out from his strange experience in the taxi right up to what he had seen in the museum. Far from thinking him odd, she was absolutely fascinated by what he told her. Although like Halim she had studied history she did not believe that history could provide a rational explanation or a context for every current event. Unexplained phenomena were unsettling to Halim, but for Petya they were both exciting and intriguing.

Suddenly Halim leapt to his feet.

"Oh my God! Tim! I should have met him half an hour ago. What was I thinking of? I am so sorry. I must go. I will call you. No, I do not have your number. I, I will come to the museum again. I am sorry. I really must rush."

As he left, Halim half remembered his manners.

"It was lovely meeting you," he called back to her and in an instant he was running down Gurko Street at full speed, leaving the young lady he had invited for a coffee to pick up the bill.

Petya did not mind about the bill, but was unhappy that he had left so suddenly. Petya remained thoughtful. He certainly was an interesting young man. She hoped very much that he would keep his word and visit the museum again.

"He had better had," she said to herself under her breath.

She called the waiter over and paid for the coffees and the rather splendid cakes that Halim had ordered, although his remained untouched on the plate. The waiter gave a knowing smile as he cleared the things away and, as he headed for the kitchen, he took a huge bite from the remaining cake. Petya laughed out loud and the waiter grinned back at her unashamedly pushing the rest of the cake into his already full mouth.

Halim got to the agreed meeting place nearly forty minutes behind schedule expecting Tim to be hopping mad. At first he could not see him and feared that he might have given up and gone home, but suddenly he spotted Tim just across the street reading the information in the window of the 'Real English School'. As Tim turned he saw Halim and immediately called him across.

"This place might interest you. I don't know what a real English school is, but it seems they offer Bulgarian lessons too," Tim informed him. "They're not expensive either," he added.

Petya Licheva lay on her bed in the small apartment she shared with her elder sister, Ilina, and her husband. Originally the two sisters lived in the flat with their parents, but after their parents divorced and went their separate ways Petya and Ilina stayed on and Ilina, then nineteen, took over the tenancy. As soon as her sister got engaged Petya started looking for a place of her own. Whenever she viewed a place her sister invariably accompanied her and more often than not it was Ilina who deemed the places unsuitable. After looking at and rejecting apartment number six Ilina questioned the whole enterprise.

"Why are you looking for somewhere, Petya? Don't you like Lyudmil?"

"Of course I like him, you know I do," Petya maintained, "But you are getting married in three months. You don't want your little sister hanging around," she added emphatically.

"That's just it. I don't want you to go. This has been our home since we were children. You belong here."

Petya looked at her sister in amazement. "If it were me getting married I would shove you out without a thought," Petya told her. "The idea of all three of us living here is ridiculous."

However, ridiculous or not that is what they did and so far it had worked out very well. Ilina and Lyudmil had a relationship that Petya admired. They were very close, but not in a way that excluded others and Petya was surprisingly comfortable with the arrangement. Petya was lying there staring at the ceiling deep in thought. Perhaps living with a couple who got on so well made her more discerning about her own relationships. Despite her good looks it was some time since Petya's last involvement with a man. The truth was that she got easily bored and her last boyfriend had ended up on the scrap heap like all the previous ones. Her feelings for the unfortunate young man had just dwindled away. Usually she had the decency to tell them how she felt, but on the last occasion she had simply stopped responding to Dimitar's overtures. After a week of her not returning his texts or answering the phone to him he got the message and gave up trying to contact her. At the time this had annoyed her; surely she was worth a bit of effort, but now she just looked back on his lack of persistence as pathetic.

Dimitar was just one more in a long sequence of stupid, selfish boys, most of whom were better off staying with their mothers. Somewhere along the line she did have a brief fling with an ex tutor who she had become reacquainted with at an event organised by the museum. He was nearly twenty years older than her, but his level of maturity was more to her liking. However, seeing him naked put an end to the affair. Although the young men she had previously dated were emotionally like Neanderthals they did all have nice bodies. She was not yet ready for a man with wrinkly bits.

The young guy she had met today was something else entirely. He was not only very handsome he also had a vitality that she found really attractive. He was lively and earnest, qualities that made him interesting to be with. Petya smiled to herself, thinking how she would have reacted if Dimitar, or one of his predecessors, had rushed away in the manner in which Halim had earlier that day. She would have dropped them instantly. With Halim it simply added to the intrigue. She wanted this man. Petya closed her eyes in order to think nice thoughts. She very much hoped that he would turn up at the museum again as he had promised. On further reflection, she was sure that he would.

At the same time that Petya had been lying on her bed mooning over Halim, the subject of her thoughts had been in an equally pensive mood. Although Halim did think about Petya it was more as a result of his guilt at treating her with such a lack of manners. In particular, he was mortified that he had left her to pick up the bill at the restaurant. In Turkey this would have been unspeakable behaviour and he had no wish to treat a very charming Bulgarian girl with any less respect. He had already resolved to return to the museum at the earliest opportunity to apologise to her. However, having decided on a course of action to put that matter right, his mind had now moved on to consider the 'discoveries' he had made at the museum.

After five minutes of trying to make sense of it all, Halim decided that he would have to approach the matter more methodically. As an historian he had learned to collect and record all the facts, put them together with existing knowledge from the time and then establish hypotheses that might provide an explanation. Halim took out his notepad and listed all the unusual things that had occurred since his arrival. Firstly there were his initial feelings that the surroundings of Arbanasi were familiar to him. Secondly there was the vision of the old house alongside the oak tree and the substantial fact of the oak tree's continued existence. Thirdly there was his discovery in the museum that the house he had seen in his mind's eye was an accurate depiction of a village house from the early or middle period of Ottoman rule, possibly from earlier. Lastly there was the artist's impression of a scene from seventeenth century Arbanasi that actually showed the house alongside the oak tree exactly as he had seen it.

Halim re-read his list of events and although a great deal of it could be explained, some things remained for the time being beyond his comprehension. However, he tried to reassure himself that this was normal at an early stage of investigation. He started with the artist's impression of Arbanasi in the seventeenth century. Like the oak tree this drawing existed. He had seen it and studied it. He had not noticed when the drawing was made, but for the time being he could assume it was done in modern times. It was common for museums nowadays to include drawings of this kind to help visitors in forming an accurate impression of how things had been. The artist's depiction of peasant houses of the time appeared to be accurate as one would expect and there was no reason to be surprised at seeing the oak tree in the picture. The artist would, whilst compiling his drawing, have visited Arbanasi and could well have included the oak tree as a result of this research. Oak trees stood for centuries and the artist would therefore have felt safe in replicating the tree exactly in his drawing. Halim had no doubt that if he looked at the drawing again he would find other features of the village as it was today that had also been replicated by the artist, the contours of the landscape, for example, or the layout of the roads and paths.

This was all logical as far as it went, but the thing that eluded explanation was his ability to see this house in his mind's eye without any prior knowledge of what houses in seventeenth century Bulgaria looked like. Add this to his feelings on arriving in the village that he had been here before and he had to admit that he still had a mystery on his hands. Halim thought back to his time at university when he had studied the Tarnovo uprising and asked himself whether his research might have included a brief study of how people lived and were housed. He was sure it had not and, although he had seen pictures of Arbanasi, during his time as a student and again just before he came here, the pictures had only been of the monasteries and historical sites and certainly not of the approach to the village. Anyway, even if he had seen pictures of the road from Veliko Tarnovo as it approached Arbanasi, this could not have accounted for the intensity of his feeling that he knew the place intimately.

Halim started to consider why he had been so interested in the second Tarnovo uprising in the late seventeenth century, especially given that most respected historical opinion wrote it off as mere legend. For the first time he began to see why his tutor, Dr Sadik, had found his interest in it so baffling. Up until now he had tried to write off his startling visions of the last few days as resulting from his avid interest in the place and its history, but all of a sudden his perspective changed. His obsession with this particular piece of history was strange and fitted together with the vision of the house and his feelings of familiarity with Arbanasi. There was no point fighting it; all of these things pointed inextricably to the conclusion that he had indeed been here before and even that he had a strong connection to Arbanasi. Halim was familiar with the saying 'when you have eliminated the impossible, whatever remains, however improbable, must be the truth.' As no other explanation presented itself he would work on the assumption that he had somehow been in Arbanasi before and would seek answers as to when and why. His first port of call would be his father.

Chapter Seven

Momchil's first week as a regular working man had gone like a dream. According to his cousin Vladimir this had been the busiest week since he had bought the van and started up his 'Man with a Van' business. It seemed that their first job, the successful delivery of the sofa from the large furniture store on the outskirts of the city to the house in Gurko Street, had opened the floodgates and this one store alone had given them ten more jobs during the course of the week. On Wednesday they had picked up four items at once from the furniture store and by lunchtime had delivered all four items to four different addresses without a hitch. Only an hour ago as they finished for the weekend Vladimir had taken Momchil aside and told him that it would never have been possible without him. His chest had puffed up with pride and he had given his elder cousin one of his special hugs. His biggest hug of all was of course reserved for his little sister. He knew only too well how much he owed her for making it all possible, but as usual when he tried to thank her she brushed his gratitude aside.

"What we do we do together, Momchil. We are a team," she asserted.

If such a thing were possible he loved her even more. Maybe he could not see his sister, but he understood more than anyone how beautiful Denitsa was.

Denitsa, having recovered from Momchil's fraternal hug, had retired to her room to get ready for the evening. Vladimir had invited Denitsa and Momchil to dinner at one of the many restaurants in Arbanasi to celebrate their first week of working together and she was very much looking forward to it. This would be the first time that Denitsa had eaten out in the company of young people, her only previous experience of eating in restaurants being family occasions with her mother and Uncle Nedyalko. Vladimir had also announced with a touch of intrigue that a female friend had asked to join them too. Denitsa had spent half the day speculating on who this could be and what her relationship was with her cousin. It was only when Vladimir, unable to contain himself any longer, had blurted out that the young woman had already met Denitsa that she guessed who it must be. Other than clients of Vladimir's business, the only young woman she had met was the rather impressive Galena from the field. She hoped very much it would be her.

As Denitsa thought about meeting Galena again the whole business of the previous Sunday and the strange series of events came flooding back to her. During the week she had been so busy she had hardly had time to give any thought to it all. Also she was so enjoying her time here in Arbanasi, she did not want anything to interfere with her feeling of well-being. Nevertheless she had now let the thoughts enter her mind and suddenly she found herself unable to focus on anything else. Again in her mind's eye she saw the body of the young man on the ground with her, or at least someone that looked like her, bent over him. As before she could not see the face of the young man clearly and had no idea who he was. She recalled the sounds before she passed out and her assertion that some sort of battle was taking place.

Denitsa tried to push these images away and instead found herself thinking about her meeting with Galena which was more tangible and not at all distressing. She thought also about her conviction that the field and the road leading to it were familiar to her and that she had often been there, indeed had worked there. These thoughts did not distress her either. Oddly she regarded these as facts for which an explanation would arise. Galena was the key and she now believed it significant that Galena had asked to be included in the evening's festivities. It was quite possible that Galena held a candle for Vladimir. Who could blame her? He was a good looking and now very eligible young man. However, Denitsa was suddenly certain that it was because of her that Galena had invited herself to eat with them that evening.

Looking up from her thoughts Denitsa saw the clock on the wall and was alarmed to discover that she had only thirty minutes left to get ready. She grabbed her things and headed for the bathroom. Her brother Momchil still found the shower in Vladimir's bathroom a luxurious novelty and all week he had spent hours standing under it. She could only hope that he had already completed his ablutions and left the bathroom free and relatively dry. Otherwise she would be keeping everyone waiting including Galena and this she most certainly wanted to avoid. However, she intended to look her best tonight and even if it meant making everyone late, she was not going to be rushed. If her cousin thought her pretty, he had not seen anything yet!

Galena was also anticipating the evening with curiosity and relish. She was sitting in front of her mother's dressing table, the only one in the house, brushing her thick hair with a wooden handled brush that had belonged to her grandmother. Unusually she had decided to wear her hair down. For all sorts of reasons she wanted to look her best and she knew that she was more eye catching with her hair falling loosely over her shoulders. Denitsa's belief that Galena may have feelings for her cousin was not so much inaccurate as misplaced. Galena had known Vladimir for most of her life and she did regard him as an attractive man. However, he had passed up many opportunities to ask her out and was not going to do so now. Consequently she had long since ceased to think of him in this way. Nevertheless, she enjoyed his company and the opportunity to meet his cousin again added some considerable interest to the evening. In a way that Galena could not explain she had felt a closeness to Denitsa that was odd given the brief nature of their encounter. It was as if she had always known her which she patently had not. Then there was Denitsa's big lump of a brother who Vladimir now spoke of with real affection. Only a few weeks ago Vladimir had told her about his blind cousin coming to work for him as if he was the victim of some sort of family conspiracy, but now his perspective had changed completely and he could not praise Momchil enough. It all made for an entertaining evening.

Vladimir only had one concern about the evening. The week he had spent in the company of his beautiful young cousin had been a rare pleasure and increasingly he had found himself fighting off feelings about her that were not entirely appropriate. He was sure that she had picked this up and had seemed at first to be a little disconcerted. However, as the week wore on she became more mischievous and seemed intent on gently teasing him. Today in particular she had been having fun at his expense.

"Don't think I always go around in old jeans and baggy tee-shirts, Vladimir. Now you have invited me out I hope you are ready for the transformation," she had declared earlier.

"I am sure you will look lovely and that I will be very proud of you," he had replied rather stiffly.

However, his worry was that being proud of his cousin may not be his paramount reaction when the 'transformed' Denitsa appeared for the evening. He would just have to cope as best he could. Of course having Galena there as well, a girl who almost made a profession out of teasing people, would certainly not make it any easier.

Halim also had a pleasant evening planned. Margot and Tim had invited him to a new pizza restaurant in Veliko Tarnovo that they had been to a few times and really liked. Earlier in the week he had visited the museum again to make his peace with the young assistant, Petya. He was nervous about meeting her again after his shameful behaviour, but he need not have worried. He was taken aback to find that, far from being put out, she seemed genuinely pleased to see him. It appeared that she had been expecting him.

Rather without thinking he had found himself asking her out which Petya had immediately consented to. Halim had hoped to get across to her that he just wanted to be friends, two young historians with things in common, but somehow Petya made that impossible. Halim asked himself why he was so reluctant to get more involved with her, she was after all a gorgeous young woman with lots to say. Thinking about it he realised it was her intensity that made him hesitate. It was as if he was in danger of being entirely consumed by her, although he could not easily say what it was that Petya did or said that made him think that. Certainly it was not what he was used to in Turkey.

From Halim's point of view the invitation from Tim and Margot had fitted perfectly into his plan of keeping distance between them and, having squared it with Margot, his intention was to collect Petya and join his British hosts for an enjoyable evening together. He was sure they would all get on well and it would be an opportunity for Petya to practice her English which he was sure she would welcome. Halim was a little surprised when Margot suggested it may not be the type of evening that Petya was hoping for, but he was adamant that she would be delighted to meet them. Margot was not so sure. She thought back to when she was young and could not recall ever having been asked out by a young man as good looking as Halim. However, she was quite certain that had she been she would not have wanted to spend the first date in the company of two middle aged strangers. Perhaps it was his Muslim sense of propriety that led him to conclude that he and Petya should be chaperoned. She decided it was his business and said nothing more.

Vladimir was sitting in the kitchen chatting away to Momchil, trying to divert his thoughts away from Denitsa. He had booked the table for seven thirty and was just starting to get a little anxious about the time when he heard Denitsa approaching. The door opened and his cousin shyly entered the room. All her teasing bravado had left her and she behaved more like a young girl about to go to her first prom.

She wore a dark blue cotton dress, sleeveless, knee length and very plain and through its simplicity showing off her perfectly shaped arms and slim figure. On her small feet she wore silver strappy sandals with a surprising three inch heel. She had put her hair up in a loose bun, not expertly so that some tendrils of hair escaped around her face. She wore silver earrings in the shape of small hearts, a family heirloom passed to her by her grandmother. Three silver bangles adorned her left arm. Her make-up was simple, a touch of black mascara and red lipstick.

Vladimir looked intently without staring, taking in the detail without being seen to do so. At that moment he knew. This beauty was not intended for some mundane affair, was too fine for base instincts. She was intended for something higher, to be part of a love that normal mortals will never know or even aspire to and that will transcend the normal accepted meaning of love. And also at that moment his silly male thoughts dissipated into thin air to be replaced by the love and admiration properly felt by an elder cousin. After all his fears he was first and foremost proud to call her family.

Momchil felt it all too. The shyness of her entrance; the change in the atmosphere that her entrance engendered; the electricity in the air that energised the room; the sharp intake of breath that informed him that something special had happened. His sister's appearance in the room changed everything, perhaps forever.

It was an enchanted evening in early summer in a picturesque village in one of the prettiest parts of Bulgaria. The sun shone late on the streets of Arbanasi. Tim was waiting for Margot to get ready, sitting in the back garden with a beer. Halim was standing in the living room by the window also waiting. As he stood there looking out, the family from next door came out of their house and walked towards the sunlight sinking slowly into the west. He had only seen her once before from a distance in Gurko Street a week earlier, but he saw her again now. Was it a trick of the light as she walked towards the sun or was it something in his own imagination? Before his eyes the scene changed and she became the only person on the street that evening; everyone else seemed to vanish. He was dimly aware that the church clock was chiming the hour as if announcing her. As Halim looked at Denitsa, she turned her head and looked back over her shoulder, her dark brown eyes momentarily locked onto his and seemed to bore into him seeking his very soul. He found himself being transported to a new place, to a new level of feeling. He felt as if he no longer belonged to himself and in a subtle way he was right. When their eyes met, unbeknown to him the control of the onward direction of his life, one could even say control of his destiny, passed from him to her.

Chapter Eight

It had been an eventful evening and an enjoyable one. It had left Vladimir with a great deal to think about. When there was thinking to be done Vladimir liked to be alone and undisturbed. The best way he knew to achieve this was by taking a long walk into the surrounding hills and this was what he was doing now. Armed with just a bottle of mineral water and a thick crust of bread he was soon three kilometres from the village heading upwards. The morning sun was strong and he could feel its heat on his uncovered head. Vladimir did not worry about this as he knew that within ten minutes he would enter the forest and could rely on natural shade for as long as he wanted to continue walking. He felt good and was not planning to turn back any time soon.

The story told by Denitsa had been mind blowing. Vladimir's strong impression was that Denitsa intended to tell only Galena about her experiences since coming to Arbanasi. She had seemed to be trying to engineer a situation where she could have a private conversation with Galena, but given how they were seated at the restaurant this was never really possible. Vladimir himself had not understood why she was doing this and he had started to get irritated by it. Denitsa had suddenly seemed to realise that she was in danger of upsetting her cousin. She could see that it was neither practical nor polite to speak only with Galena and had boldly announced to everyone that she had something to tell them. Galena had immediately seemed intrigued whereas Momchil looked terrified. Vladimir was just glad that they were all going to be party to whatever it was she wanted to say.

When she started to relate all that had happened to her on her first Sunday in Arbanasi everyone fell silent. As she told the story about her walk to the field that felt so familiar and her strong feelings of attachment to the piece of land Denitsa had looked at Galena hoping for some comment from her, but she had remained silent. Even when Denitsa revealed that she seemed to know Galena still the local girl said nothing. Without a word from anyone, but amid looks of alarm and fascination, Denitsa continued on to tell of her experiences on the road to Veliko Tarnovo. Suddenly Momchil had not been able to bear the tension any longer.

"What does all this mean? It is starting to frighten me. Has no one anything to say?"

Galena had looked at Momchil and reached forward a hand, placing it gently on his arm as if to reassure, but also to quieten him.

Momchil had read the intent correctly and fell silent. Galena cleared her throat and looking from one to another had begun to speak.

"As you, Vladimir, know I am an only child, but as a small girl I always had a notion that somehow somewhere I had a sister. This feeling was sometimes overwhelming and I often spoke of it to my mother who as far as I recall never gave me any encouragement in this belief. As I got older it became clear to me that this talk grieved my mother greatly. I became aware that she had desperately wanted more children, but this had never proved possible. Even now I do not know the reason for this. Seeing how my apparent fancy regarding a mythical sister was upsetting my mother I resolved to talk about it no more and slowly it became less real in my own mind. However, there have been times over the last couple of years when new friends have asked me whether I have any brothers or sisters and I have found myself saying that I have one sister. Friends often seemed curious why I said yes and then gave no further details about her, but I never went down this road. In my mind I had not told a lie, because I believed it to be so. By embroidering the story with invented or imagined details I would indeed have made a lie of it and so after saying I had a sister I remained silent on the subject."

Vladimir had been confused. "Galena, why do you tell us this. You may have wanted a sister, but as you said at the start, you are an only child. What are we supposed to make of this?"

"Make of it what you will, Vladimir. I only tell you what I believe, even though it would seem to be impossible. I am simply putting this alongside what Deni has told us. Do you not believe her either?" Galena had asked. "Denitsa's story shows us that not everything can be so easily explained."

Vladimir walked on, his stride quickening to match his racing thoughts. Nothing made sense and he had been grappling with that stark fact all morning. Finally he had been forced to come to the same conclusion as Galena: not everything in life could be explained logically. Denitsa was sure she was connected to the field where Galena's family worked the land, but she wasn't. Galena was sure she had a sister, but she clearly did not. He looked up to the heavens in the hope of some enlightenment and indeed some sort of explanation did present itself. Have we all lived a previous life? He had heard this notion before and indeed Vladimir was dimly aware that it was central to the beliefs of some religions. He had never given the idea any credence or to be more accurate he had not ever given much thought to it. Perhaps he should now.

Just as Vladimir's thoughts on the subject were finding a degree of equilibrium his mind moved on to thinking about Galena herself. While she had been speaking on the previous evening he had legitimately had the opportunity to look at her. He had studied the girl as well as paying attention to what she was saying. How had he never before seen her beauty? Momchil was blind, but he had perceived it, whereas Vladimir with perfect sight had overlooked it for years. Suddenly he had been knocked over by her, not only by her physical beauty, but also by her sensitivity and her empathy. All were part of the whole that was Galena. Also for the first time he had realised that she had feelings for him. When she looked at him it was as if she was seeking some kind of answer and with it he had perceived some bewilderment on her part.

"Why do you not notice me?" she seemed to be asking. Well, he had noticed her now!

*

Petya tried hard to be angry with Halim, but all she could feel was an intense disappointment. She had so been looking forward to their evening together and was completely thrown when she discovered that it was to be spent in the company of his British hosts. It was made harder by the fact that they were so nice, making it impossible to blame them for her disappointment. Indeed in other circumstances she would have found their company delightful, but not tonight. Halim's naïve assertions that the evening provided her with a good opportunity to practice her English just made it all the more painful. What she wanted was some time alone with Halim for whom her feelings were getting slightly out of control. She was sure that Margot had accurately picked up what was going on and she had done her best to find a reason to leave early, but the stupid men were having none of it. They were having a great time and were typically unaware that for some the evening was not what had been hoped for.

On top of everything else Halim had from time to time seemed quite distracted. Although he had clearly been enjoying the evening, every so often his thoughts seemed to drift away.

"Penny for them!" Margot had said at one point, which was not a phrase that she or Halim had heard before, but Tim set them right with an excruciatingly long explanation.

After that Petya had herself employed the phrase on a couple of occasions when Halim's attention seemed elsewhere. He had on both occasions made light of it, teasing her about her use of the newly learned English idiom.

"Perhaps if you offered me a lev for my thoughts, I might tell you what they are," he had said. "A penny is not very much."

She had laughed it off and had assumed he was still wondering about his strange experiences since coming to Bulgaria. Just to make matters worse Tim had insisted on giving her a lift home and Halim left with Tim and Margot without even getting out of the car!

What was she to do now? She desperately wanted to contact Halim and arrange to meet him, but she still had some pride left. No, she would just have to wait for him to contact her and if he didn't, well he would live to regret it. She would not forget about him. In fact, she was starting to realise that forgetting about Halim would be very hard indeed.

Tim had been up early and had started marking out his proposed vegetable patch. Although it was Saturday Halim appeared for work at eight as usual, having asked Margot at breakfast if he could swap his days and have Monday off. By the time Halim joined Tim he was ready to start digging it over. He had two spades and a garden fork at the ready. Tim hated digging. As the one time owner of a fleet of mechanical diggers it always seemed such a ridiculous waste of effort. Still, it was a beautiful morning and soon the two of them were hard at work. As with other jobs it quickly became clear that Halim could work considerably faster than Tim, but then Tim reasoned he was less than half his age. At first they chatted away merrily without their work being affected, but as the sun beat down Tim started to flag and was soon conducting his side of the conversation leaning on his spade. In little more than half an hour Tim was getting fed up and soon sloped away for what he regarded as a well-earned coffee break. No such invitation was extended to Halim who anyway seemed perfectly content to continue digging over the plot.

In truth he was glad to be alone as he had a great deal on his mind. As Petya had suspected on the previous evening he was still preoccupied with all the strange things that were happening to him, but beyond this there was now the girl. It was his neighbour's cousin more than anything else that crowded his thoughts. He had seen her only briefly the previous evening as the family left to go out for the night and he had been overawed by her timeless beauty. She moved with such grace he had been unable to take his eyes off her and for a brief moment she had looked back at him returning his gaze with devastating results. Halim's heart had raced and his legs had turned to jelly. From his vantage point by the window, he had continued to watch her until she turned down a side street and out of sight. Now as he tried to carry on working on the vegetable plot Halim again felt his legs going weak. He steadied himself against the side of the garden shed and closed his eyes as he tried to recapture in his mind the magical essence of the girl. Instead it was her image that captured him.

Halim had seen many beautiful girls in his time both at home in Turkey and here in Bulgaria. Indeed Petya with whom he had spent the previous evening could properly be described as beautiful. This girl was more than that; she was bewitching. He had not even spoken to her and yet in some strange way he could not explain Halim felt drawn to her. Somehow her presence seemed to give meaning to all the experiences he had been grappling with since his arrival in Arbanasi.

His reverie was broken by the sudden appearance of Margot brandishing a cup of coffee.

"Please excuse my husband's manners," she said. "He slunk off for a coffee without even offering you one. He can be a right little toad at times."

Halim had no idea what a toad was, but instinctively felt he should not agree too enthusiastically.

"It is OK," he replied. "He was probably thirsty after starting so early. I have not done much yet."

"Tim is always thirsty," Margot countered. "But never thirsty enough to drink water. A constant diet of coffee and beer will be his downfall one of these days."

Halim was on the verge of adding that Tim appeared to quite like wine too, but thought better of it.

"Coffee can be very welcome when one is working. Thank you."

Margot gave him a wry smile and went back to the house, leaving Halim to return to his thoughts.

Halim had asked for Monday off so that he could return to the museum to continue his research. It would also give him an opportunity to see Petya again. He really liked her and had found her company very engaging, but he remained wary of her. He had certainly benefited from talking to her about his feelings of familiarity with Arbanasi and about his vision of the house. Although Petya was also an historian it was clear to him that her thought processes were completely different to his own. In some ways she appeared to him as a superior thinker as she was open to a much wider set of explanations. He was sure that she would be able to help him get to the bottom of everything. However, he was nervous about contacting her because she seemed to interpret any approach from him as more significant than he intended. Nevertheless, he could not solve any of the riddles currently confronting him without visiting the museum again. He had asked for Monday off for the expressed purpose of going to the museum and that is what he would do and when there he would ask for Petya's assistance.

There and then he decided to ring her to check that she was working on Monday. She assured him that she was and said she could not wait to see him which Halim thought was nice, but again it made him nervous. It was in fact Petya's day off, but she immediately rang her colleague and friend Desi to swap shifts. Desi received the request with a knowing smile.

"Are we expecting the handsome Turk?" she enquired.

Much to Desi's surprise Petya snapped at her.

"Why are you so interested in him? I'm sure he is not interested in you."

For a moment Desi did not reply. Her friend had never spoken to her in that way before and it upset her. However, she was not going to start trading insults on the phone.

"Well, maybe you'll be lucky and he will turn up out of the blue," she said.

"It is possible. He is very interested in our work at the museum," her friend replied.

"I am sure you will have a very interesting day," said Desi and left it at that.

As she put her phone down Petya realised she had been really off hand with her friend. Why had she spoken to her like that, in that stupid jealous way? She thought about ringing back, but feared she may make it worse.

Later that day, Halim called his father. He had not properly spoken to him since arriving and although he would never say so his father would be worrying about him. His original intention had been to tell his father all about his experiences since arriving in Arbanasi and to ask him if he had ever visited the area as a child. However, he now instinctively knew that any explanation lay elsewhere. Instead he talked about his lovely host family, the beauty of the region and the glorious weather. His father was glad to hear that everything was going well.

*

By the time he arrived at the forest, Vladimir was starting to feel the heat of the sun on his uncovered head. He turned into the shade of the trees and following a familiar path he started to increase his stride. He had walked about two kilometres along the forest path when his attention was taken by the sound of goats bleating. Vladimir was aware that goats most commonly bleat to communicate between mother and kids and this was what it sounded like now. At first he was sure that it was the sound of young goats that he was hearing although at times it sounded more like a crying human child. Becoming a little uncertain he changed course and leaving the shade of the forest he walked across the hills in the direction of the sound. As he drew closer and could see the goats with their young in the distance the sound seemed to merge with a human voice crying mournfully. As far as he could see the goats appeared unattended and he worried that the shepherd could be lying injured nearby.

Ignoring the intense heat of the day Vladimir started to run towards the tribe of goats. As he did so the sound of the bleating goats gave way to a distinctly human voice, but as he arrived on the scene there was nobody to be seen although the mournful voice continued. The voice seemed to be coming from below the ground. He feared that although the earth did not seem to have been disturbed, that someone was buried alive. He knew this to be irrational, but then nothing else was making sense. Now feeling very concerned Vladimir started digging furiously using some old slates that were lying nearby as a spade and when this proved an inefficient tool he used his bare hands. In no time his hands were scratched and bleeding, but suddenly he felt something under the earth. He dug even more furiously than before and as an object wrapped in cloth revealed itself the voice suddenly ceased. Vladimir carefully lifted the object from the ground and removed the soiled cloth. In his hands he held a silver container which he opened to reveal an icon of the Virgin Mary, perfectly preserved.

Chapter Nine

Uncle Nedyalko was bored. He hated Sundays in the village because unless you were a church-goer there was nothing to do. Almost all of the other men in the village were under the control of their wives and so most of the small bars that he and his friends frequented stood empty. He had got up late as he often did so that there were not too many hours to fill in the day, but this meant that he had already missed breakfast at his sister's house. Rada would already be making her way to church with the other old crones from the village.

When her husband Nicholai had been alive she had never bothered about attending Sunday services yet now she never missed. Nedyalko knew his sister well and realised that she too was often bored and lonely and that attending church gave her a purpose and also an opportunity to gossip with her friends. Also she believed that as a widow she should from time to time put her grief on display and going to church every Sunday dressed in her widow's weeds was one way of doing this. Whenever Nedyalko questioned why she went to church or tried to remind her that she and Nicholai were never devout, his sister went all pious on him, claiming it was only Nicholai's membership of the Communist Party that had prevented her from attending church regularly. Nedyalko was aware that Nicholai's interest in politics was yet another myth. Both he and Nicholai had joined the local party for one reason only: the mayor liked a drink and his home distilled rakia was known to flow freely at party meetings. Still, he had long since given up talking to his sister on these matters. If she wanted to believe that she had always been a God fearing woman married to a local political hero who was he to spoil it for her?

Nevertheless he did feel a little neglected and to make matters worse she had recently told him that she thought Sunday dinner to be a pointless meal without her beloved Nicholai to share it with her. Consequently, Nedyalko didn't even have that to look forward to. Suddenly he had an idea. As an act of kindness to his sister and to pass the day tolerably he would offer to take her to Arbanasi to see her children. It was clear to him that even after just a week she was missing them terribly and he possessed the only means for her to get there, the old Trabant. Impressed by his own gallantry, Nedyalko tidied himself up and headed towards the church with the intention of speaking to his sister as soon as the service was over.

He did not have long to wait. After about ten minutes he spotted his sister, Rada leaving the service with one of her friends. To his surprise he noticed that she was not dressed in black, but had on her best bib and tucker. Immediately she saw the Trabant parked outside the church she went over to speak to her brother.

With no prompting from him she found herself explaining why she was not dressed in widow's garb as was her custom on a Sunday.

"Milena here has invited me to her home for lunch. It is her daughter's birthday and they are having a small celebration. Isn't that kind of her?"

Nedyalko agreed that it was, bravely overcoming his resentment that nobody had thought to invite him!

"That will be nice for you. It is good of you to think of my sister, Milena," he said, addressing the friend directly.

Then turning back to his sister he added, "In which case you won't be interested in my plan to visit Arbanasi, will you?"

At once he could see that his sister was in a dilemma. Nedyalko felt a touch of guilt, even selfishness, that he had still mentioned his plan despite the fact that Rada had a nice day planned already. He could easily have left it to next week. Milena too could sense her friend's indecision.

"That is a lovely idea and you have been so missing them, left on your own and all. You are of course welcome at my house for my girl's birthday, but I am sure you would prefer to spend the day with your own daughter and of course with Momchil and your nephew."

Rada looked imploringly at Milena. "You are sure you will not be offended?" she asked and was immediately reassured.

"Of course not. Off you go! You are already dressed for the occasion."

Rada kissed her friend and, as far as she could still jump, jumped into her brother's old car. Right away she started dialling her daughter's number. As she waited for Denitsa to answer she turned to Nedyalko and smiled.

"You heard Milena. Off you go!"

In reply Nedyalko put the old Trabant into gear and in a plume of black smoke roared away.

By the time they arrived lunchtime was approaching and Nedyalko was hoping that his nephew had received enough notice to conjure up a good meal as he had on the previous occasion. He was not disappointed and as he and his sister entered the house they were met with a delicious smell that Nedyalko instantly recognised as pork kebapche. He could already imagine himself seated at the table with a glass of cold Bulgarian beer, hopefully Zagorka, waiting for the kebapche to be served with fried potatoes. Rada was overwhelmed with joy at the sight of her children and could see at once that the three cousins were getting along famously. As a further surprise her sister, Vladimir's mother, was also there to greet her. She felt content and soon she too was looking forward to lunch.

At the table Denitsa was gushing in her praise of both her cousin and her brother, Momchil.

"You should see them, Mama. They are the best furniture removers Veliko Tarnovo has ever seen. The work is flooding in and soon our dear cousin will be a rich man and much he deserves it, doesn't he Momchil?"

Momchil settled back to deliver a tribute to Vladimir, but before he could open his mouth Denitsa was off again.

"Maybe the lord is already rewarding him. You won't believe what he found in the hills yesterday. Tell them, Vlado!"

Vladimir started to tell the story of the sounds he had heard while walking in the forest which had led him to the spot where the icon was buried. However, his tale was too drawn out for Denitsa's liking and she soon interrupted to finish the story herself.

Having concluded the tale Denitsa rushed from the table and returned with the precious icon in its silver repousse cover. As she removed the cover to reveal the ancient icon of the Virgin Mary her mother and uncle instinctively crossed themselves. Rada stared in wonder and amazement, but Uncle Nedyalko's initial piety did not last very long.

"It must be worth a fortune!" he exclaimed. "The question is how could you sell it and who would offer you a good price. I have a friend who…."

"Be quiet, Nedyalko before you completely disgrace yourself," his sister interjected. "It is a holy icon of which you speak. Show some respect before you are struck down."

At this warning Nedyalko gave an involuntary glance upwards. He decided it would be best to hold his tongue, for now at least.

For about an hour the family continued the conversation about what to do with the icon that the three cousins had been engaged in all day. Uncle Nedyalko made one more abortive attempt to lead his family into temptation, but his ideas fell on deaf ears. Finally it was agreed that the mayor should be consulted. Vladimir went off to phone him and within five minutes he was back.

"He is on his way round," he informed everyone. "He made me describe the icon in detail and the circumstances in which it was found and then said it is potentially a very important find. He also started to tell me that there is a legend surrounding it, but I suggested he saw it first to be sure. He will be here in ten minutes."

Uncle Nedyalko opened his mouth to speak, but his sister was on him at once.

"When the mayor gets here don't you dare talk about selling the icon. This is an honourable family and we will do what is right. Is that clear?"

It was only too clear to Nedyalko although he thought they were passing up an opportunity that would never come again. However, he held his peace.

Hristo Genkov, the mayor of Arbanasi, was an imposing figure. He was more than six feet tall with broad shoulders and an upright frame. He was not the sort of man that one would pick an argument with unless your cause was just. In fact Hristo gave his villagers little reason to argue with him. The mayor was also a devout man. He lived up to his name Hristo and carried Christ in his heart. Like his father before him, he had been mayor for more than twenty years and was loved and respected in his village. Unlike some of his counterparts in other districts he had never used his position to further his own interests, but had dealt with every situation with fairness and integrity. As a young man he had often thought of becoming a priest within the Orthodox Church, but had been worried about the compromises that life under Communism would require of him. In the end he had turned away from this course, but had remained deeply religious.

Hristo was now nearly seventy and had been starting to find the responsibilities of office arduous. Besides that he had seven grandchildren and wanted to spend as much time as possible with them. His eldest grandson, Deyan, shared his passion for football and was developing into a decent player. Deyan's father had no interest in sport and Hristo wanted to be there to encourage the boy.

His wife, thinking only of him, had recently been encouraging Hristo to retire. He had been taking her advice seriously and on one level had been inclined to follow it. In truth he was held back by concerns over who would succeed him. The most likely candidate was Kaloyan Radkov, a so-called businessman whom Hristo regarded as little more than a crook. Many of the young men in the village were impressed by Radkov's conspicuous shows of wealth and would no doubt vote for him. Most of the older folk were less sure of him, but would probably do nothing to prevent his election. In any case if the outcome seemed in doubt Radkov would not be adverse to a little persuasion. For this reason Hristo had dithered over his decision. Now with this news from Vladimir he was glad he was still mayor and able to deal with it appropriately.

He replaced the receiver and turned to his wife, his eyes sparkling with joy and passion.

"My dear, I have just been told the most incredible news. From what I can make out young Vladimir has uncovered the ancient icon of the Virgin Mary. I asked him to describe it and how he found it. It fitted in every detail with the old legend. I am going there now."

His wife looked at him solemnly. Like her husband she was familiar with the legend of the icon of the Virgin Mary.

"Husband, Christ will surely bless you and go with you. May he bless you with his wisdom."

With his wife's words to guide him Hristo set off on the short walk to Vladimir's house. He did not know Vladimir well, but he came from a good family. Hristo had no doubt that the whole story was genuine. As he approached the front door of Vladimir's home his excitement rose. Showing as usual impeccable manners, Vladimir was waiting at the door to greet him.

"Come in, Mayor, come in! Will you drink a glass of rakia with us?"

"That would be grand" the mayor replied, "But first to business. I am very anxious to see the icon."

"Of course," said Vladimir. "It is on the dining room table surrounded by my family. I think they are frightened it will disappear as mysteriously as it arrived."

Hristo smiled politely and followed his host into the dining room.

The mayor was greeted with warmth and respect by the family and the offers of hospitality were repeated and again politely declined. Hristo, whilst greeting everyone, could not tear his eyes away from the object on the table. This is what he had come to see. On enquiry,

Vladimir confirmed that he had found the object buried, wrapped in cloth. Hristo was overwhelmed at the sight of the icon and he gave a prayer of thanks that it had been delivered intact to people of this village. The icon belonged in Arbanasi. However, it was the silver cover that he spent most time examining. The icon had been found wrapped in cloth inside a silver repousse cover, ornamented with patterns made by hammering on the reverse side. It was the silver repousse cover spoken of in the legend that told Hristo that it was indeed the precious icon of the Virgin Mary.

"I am as sure as I can be that this is the icon referred to in the legend. It is the silver repousse cover that convinces me. It is said that the silver cover was made with the funds of a local trader whose child was cured following a pray to the icon. The icon was believed to be miraculous by both the nuns and the local people."

Vladimir's mother was the next to speak.

"I have heard this legend as a child, but had taken it as just that: a legend. Are you saying it is true, Hristo?"

The mayor did not answer the question directly, but instead started to relate the legend to the family, all of whom were listening intently.

"At the end of the fourteenth century nuns from the local convent fled Arbanasi as the Turkish invaders advanced on the village. As they left they buried the precious icon of the Virgin Mary in its silver cover wrapped in rags. According to the legend, sometime in the seventeenth century a shepherd boy heard a mournful voice coming from the ground while walking his herd in the surrounding hills, and with the help of his father found the icon where it had been buried three centuries earlier. It is believed that for a time the icon was displayed in the local church, but for several centuries its whereabouts have been a mystery. It could be that it was again buried until young Vladimir found it yesterday. The circumstances of your discovery, Vladimir, fit exactly with the legend."

After a short pause the mayor turned again to his host.

"I think I am ready for that rakia now!"

The mayor's words had a powerful effect on the assembled group, even including Nedyalko. Each one of them was overcome with wonder and astonishment, but none more so than Denitsa who became anxious and emotional. She began to speak as if involuntarily and her own words made no more sense to her than to the rest of her family who listened in awe as she spoke in staccato tones.

"Vladislav found it when he was a boy. In the hills. He gave it to the church to look after. He thought it brought him luck, but after the battle he... I don't know what he did. He was so upset. He must have buried it again. I think he loved me."

Denitsa's mother became alarmed.

"Denitsa, what are you saying? It was your cousin, Vladimir who found the icon. You know that."

"No, Vladislav was my friend. I was there. My name is.... My name is....."

"Your name is Denitsa, child. What is the matter?" her mother interrupted and as her mother became increasingly agitated, Denitsa slowly became calmer.

"Yes, my name is Denitsa, but for a moment I saw it all. I saw the icon. I saw it then in the church, but it is fading. I can't hold onto it. I want to, but I can't."

The whole family, but especially Momchil and his mother, were bewildered and anxious. Only Hristo remained in control of himself.

"It is the power of the holy icon that is at work. Do not underestimate it," he said to everyone and then he turned with compassion to Denitsa.

"Young lady, don't be alarmed. The icon is telling us what happened through you. No harm will come of it. The icon is a force for good."

Denitsa looked at him gratefully, but wanted to tell him that he only had half the story. There was more, but she could no longer reach it. She stared at the mayor silently imploring him to help her, then quite suddenly she passed out.

Chapter Ten

When Halim arrived at the museum in Veliko Tarnovo late on Monday morning he found all the staff in a state of high excitement. Earlier that day the mayor of Arbanasi had brought the holy icon to the museum, both for safe keeping and in the hope of getting it officially authenticated. All the staff were there even those like Desi who were not on the rota to work that day. Desi was the first to spot Halim and she at once approached him to tell him the news. Petya, she explained, was with the curator in the office awaiting the arrival of an official from the National Historical Museum in Sofia. They had also been told to expect the current Director of the National Historical Museum, himself an expert on the period of Ottoman rule in Bulgaria.

On hearing that his neighbour, Vladimir, was the one who had found the ancient icon, Halim was surprised that he had not heard about it. He was aware that Vladimir and Tim were very close. He expressed this surprise to Desislava.

"Apparently the mayor told the whole family to keep it to themselves until the object had been safely delivered here. By tonight the whole world will know. Petya herself is something of an expert on the Ottoman period and she and our curator are convinced it is genuine. As for the story of him being led there by a half human voice coming from below ground, well that sounds a bit far-fetched to me. I think he has been watching too many fantasy movies."

Halim remained silent. After all the strange things that had happened to him since arriving in Arbanasi he was quite prepared to believe Vladimir's tale. God knows how, but he was convinced that all these things were connected. It occurred to him that, maybe for the first time since he became a serious historian, he was prepared to accept something as true even though he had no rational explanation for it. Perhaps Petya's way of thinking was having an effect on him, broadening his mind. If he had any chance of making sense of everything then his mind needed to be open to all possibilities.

Just as he was lost in thought the main door of the museum opened and the Director of the National Historical Museum in Sofia and his full entourage of secretaries and advisors swept in. Desi and her colleagues rushed forward to greet them and seconds later Petya and the curator emerged from the office to join the welcome committee. At once she saw Halim alongside Desi. She flashed a bitter, angry look towards her friend which Desi could not comprehend. Halim was unaware of this gesture and smiled at Petya. She gave a thin-lipped smile in return. They both knew that it would be impossible to speak to each other there and then, but as far as Petya was concerned that did not matter, much as she longed for it. He had come. All that mattered now was that he had come.

*

Uncle Nedyalko had only planned to stay for the day, but since Denitsa's fainting episode on Sunday afternoon his sister had become immovable. Rada was fussing over her daughter like a mother hen and was going nowhere until she personally was sure that Denitsa was alright. Earlier that morning Rada had got up just in time to find Denitsa preparing to go to work.

"And where do you think you are going, young lady?" she had asked.

"I am going to work, Mama. I am already late. Momchil and Vlado are waiting for me."

Denitsa's mother was unimpressed. "I am surprised at the two boys for even considering it. There is only one place that you are going and that is straight back to bed."

Denitsa gave a sigh and looked to the heavens. "I am absolutely fine," she insisted. "If I do not go to work then how will Momchil manage?" she asked.

"He is a big boy. He will just have to manage. Vladimir will just have to guide him," replied her mother. "If I have to bar the door, I will. You are staying here and that is final. Anyway, we have things to discuss. I want to know exactly what has taken place since you arrived here in Arbanasi and I don't want to hear any hocus-pocus."

Then before Denitsa had the chance to protest or even to reply at all she turned on her heal and headed for the kitchen where, as she had expected, Momchil and Vladimir sat waiting. She immediately launched at them.

"I am disappointed with you two boys expecting Denitsa to work today. The girl is clearly ill. You will have to manage without her."

Momchil rose to his own and his cousin's defence.

"Mama, both of us told her she should not come to work, but she insisted she was OK."

"Don't you argue with your mother," replied Rada, not entirely reasonably. "Denitsa is staying here."

Vladimir did not want to leave a bad impression with his aunt and certainly did not want her to think him an uncaring employer, but he could see that attempts at explanation were futile. He put his hand firmly on Momchil's shoulder already much more confident with managing his cousin's disability.

"Come on cousin, let's get going. Don't worry! Remember the last time I helped you it was me that ended up on the floor. If there are any casualties today it won't be you."

They both laughed and with Vladimir's strong hand still firmly on Momchil's shoulder they rose as one and headed for the van.

Despite having already reached the age of majority and notwithstanding the fact that she was no longer living at home, Denitsa had no intention of defying her mother's authority. Her mother only ever behaved like this when she was properly worried and it was time that Denitsa told her the whole story. Her mother's concerns about Denitsa's physical health were unfounded: she was fine. However, emotionally she was a complete mess and she knew that talking to her mother, although it would increase the burden of worry on her, could only help. Consequently, by the time Rada returned to her daughter's room Denitsa was already back in bed. Denitsa's mother put her hand on her daughter's slender arm. Rada was her normal self again: sympathetic, loving and receptive. Consequently, as soon as Denitsa started to speak she burst into tears.

Nedyalko was still in bed. Usually an early riser he had remained in his room more to keep out of the way than anything else. Yesterday he had planned a nice day out with his sister, visiting her children and their sister and nephew. In his mind he had imagined an emotional welcome followed by a nice lunch with a few beers. Later in the day he had expected to drive his sister home in the early evening sunshine, a hero in her eyes. The first part of the day had gone to plan and then all hell had broken loose. He had to admit to himself that he had been shaken by events. He was not at all sure what to make of the mayor and the legend he had spoken of. He was certainly a solemn and imposing figure in whom the family had placed a great deal of trust. Nedyalko certainly admired the way he had kept his head throughout. When the mayor had suggested he could take the icon to the museum in Veliko Tarnovo the next morning they had all readily agreed. Nedyalko had suggested that as head of the family he should accompany the mayor, but his sister intervened to prevent this. She was obviously still smarting from his innocent suggestion that they should try and find a buyer for the icon, although he had long since realised the inappropriateness of this suggestion. Now they were all trying to get on with the day until the mayor reported back, probably not until the afternoon. Nedyalko regretted that he was not with him.

Nedyalko would normally have regarded all the stuff about human voices calling from beneath the earth as so much mumbo-jumbo. However, the similarities between Vladimir's reported experiences and the details of the legend itself had unnerved him. He had tried to explain it away with the assumption that Vladimir knew of the legend and his excitement at finding the icon had got the better of him, but it soon became clear that Vladimir was as ignorant about the story as he was. Then there was the odd behaviour of his beautiful and usually level-headed niece, Denitsa. When she finally passed out he had been very frightened, not only for her, but for all of them. It was as if the family, usually so reassuringly normal, had entered some dark and unfamiliar place.

Tim watched as his friend and neighbour, Vladimir helped Momchil towards the van. Twice they seemed to get their feet caught up with each other and, although neither of them ended up falling over they came mighty close a few times.

"Where's the little sister today?" Tim called over the fence. "It looks like you could do with her."

Vladimir stopped to look over at Tim, but unfortunately he had failed to give any sort of cue to Momchil who just kept on coming. Given the size of Momchil it was inevitable that Vladimir would be the one to be knocked over and soon he was sprawling on the ground. Tim was not someone to spare a friend's blushes and he laughed heartily at his neighbour's misfortune.

"Have you got a lot on today?" Tim asked as Vladimir got to his feet and brushed himself down.

Vladimir replied whilst still attending to his dirty jeans. "Yes, we have five pick-ups and deliveries, all in Tarnovo."

"Can I give you a hand? I haven't too much on today," Tim suggested.

Vladimir hesitated. Knowing that Tim was no lover of hard work he was a little suspicious of his motives.

"Are you sure or do you just want an opportunity to laugh at me?" he asked.

Tim smiled. He was giving no guarantees on that score.

"I probably will laugh at you, but you do look as if you could do with an extra pair of hands. I'll get my jacket and be with you in two minutes."

*

After delivering the precious icon to the museum in Veliko Tarnovo, Hristo decided to stay in town until he got some news from the museum staff. The curator and one of his assistants, a lovely young woman called Petya, had spent nearly two hours with him looking at the icon. In an attempt to date the artefact the young woman explained to him that they were applying the principles of typology, studying the material from which the icon and its cover were made, its form, and its most likely purpose. However, the purpose and meaning of an icon had not really changed over the centuries so they were looking to date the icon simply by looking at the materials and process used to make it. They were also checking written records from the time looking for textual clues as to which artefacts were produced during which eras. They had applied several of these techniques and were finally checking against drawings and records and against other artefacts held at the museum.

At the end of this initial process both Petya and the curator seemed to believe that the icon dated back to between 1300 and 1370. As to whether it was the icon of the legend they expressed no opinion.

"I cannot really answer that," the curator had said in response to Hristo's prompting. "We deal only in science and historical facts," he added rather pompously.

Petya on the other hand was more encouraging. "What we could say is that the mere existence of this icon coupled with the place where it was found would give support to the argument that the legend has some basis in fact."

The curator, under pressure from Hristo, nodded a reluctant assent to this suggestion.

Finally, having convinced himself that they had been presented with a genuine artefact of real historical significance, the curator said that he wanted to consult with experts from the National Historical Museum in Sofia and asked Hristo's permission to keep the icon at the museum at least until these experts could arrange to see it. Hristo agreed readily. He knew that the family would want this and anyway there was still the question of what should happen to the icon long term. For the time being it was safest to keep it at the museum.

Hristo was now sitting in a small restaurant located halfway down one of the many sets of steps that lead up and down between the various levels of the city. He was enjoying a pleasant lunch of Shopska salad followed by a bowl of Kavarma. His table was located outside allowing a panoramic view of the old town and the river Yantra. He was more than happy to sit here until the museum phoned him with some news.

*

Once Denitsa started talking the whole story poured out whilst her mother listened to her with an increasing sense of alarm. Given what a sensible girl her daughter was she was forced to take the various accounts seriously. Denitsa would never invent such a tale and she was not inclined to hallucinations or hysterical invention. Also the account from the local girl, Galena, which Denitsa also related seemed to give some credence to what her daughter had been experiencing. Rada was forced to conclude that they should consult the local priest, or better still her own priest back at home. However, she found a surprising level of resistance from Denitsa to this suggestion.

"No, Mama, I do not want that. We have already spoken to the mayor about some of this. I don't want anyone else involved. I will work it out for myself." Denitsa's manner was firm.

"But, how can you do that?" her mother asked "You need help with this Denitsa."

Her daughter shook her head and once more became agitated. Rada feared that she would pass out again, but slowly Denitsa's calm returned. She began to speak in measured tones, aware that her mother would try to rebuff what she had to say.

"Since last night I have had a lot of time to think it all through and on top of that I have had another vision as I did yesterday."

"What, about the icon?" her mother interjected.

"Partly that, yes, but I have seen myself in a different time. Galena was there as was Vladimir although he appeared younger, but their names were different. Galena was my sister."

Her mother's eyes were like saucers, but she did not interrupt. Denitsa continued.

"I was in love, wildly in love, but I could not identify the subject of my feelings. Vladimir, or Vladislav as he was called, was my closest friend, but it was not him."

Finally Rada could keep quiet no longer, her anxiety for her daughter overwhelming her and stripping her of reason.

"Stop, Denitsa! This is crazy. What could it all mean?"

"What it all means, Mama, is that I have lived before."

*

With Tim to help them the 'Man with a Van' and his unusual assistant were finished for the day at just after two o clock.

"Is it OK if I ring Halim?" Tim asked. "He is in VT somewhere. If he is ready, we could give him a lift home."

"No problem," Vladimir replied. "I'll just park up while you do it. What was he doing here?"

"He took the day off to visit the museum which just happens to be where his girlfriend works. I think he's killing two birds with one stone," replied Tim.

Vladimir pondered for a moment. "So he has gone to the museum to see his girlfriend, but also to kill birds? I don't really understand."

Tim laughed. "I'm sorry. It is another English idiom. It just means to do two things in one. He has business at the museum, but will also be able to see his girl, Petya. She is absolutely lovely."

"Of course she is lovely. All Bulgarian women are beautiful," answered Vladimir with pride.

"I can't really argue with that," said Tim and then called for hush as Halim answered his phone. Soon they were on their way to meet him outside the City Bar near the bus station.

"Shall we stop and have a drink?" Tim suggested.

Vladimir was not too fussed about the idea, but as soon as the suggestion had been translated to Momchil he gave his casting vote in Tim's favour. Vladimir parked opposite the bus station, unconcerned that it was a parking area reserved for taxis and walked away ignoring the loud hail of protests from the taxi drivers.

"It is a commercial vehicle now," he told Tim who did not care either way. His thoughts were entirely focused on getting his hands on a large beer.

As arranged Halim was waiting for them outside and soon the four of them were seated at a table waiting for their drinks, beer for Tim and Momchil and coke for Halim and Vladimir.

"So why were you at the museum?" Vladimir asked with an inward smile, ready to contradict any explanation that did not include seeing the girl.

"I am interested in the history of Arbanasi and particularly its architecture. I went there to follow up a few ideas I had, but it was impossible. The place was in uproar."

At this Vladimir's interest increased tenfold.

"Why was that?" he asked.

"You must know the answer to that," Halim replied carefully, only too aware that Vladimir had almost certainly not told Tim about the discovery of the icon.

Momchil, on the other hand had no such misgivings. "Vladimir, it must be your icon that has caused a stir. This must mean it's genuine."

Vladimir did not want to jump to any conclusions. "Let's just wait until we hear from the mayor, shall we?"

"Hang on a minute!" Tim interjected. "What the hell are you going on about?"

Momchil squeezed his cousin's arm as a sign that he intended to answer. He had been the one to let the cat out of the bag and so he would tell Tim what had happened.

Just at that moment the waitress arrived with their drinks, placing them carefully on the table. Unusually, she had been met with silence and was left to guess which drink belonged to whom. Beer for the Englishman, that bit was easy, and coke for the guy with the car keys in front of him. She was not sure if the blind man would be a drinker, but the way he wetted his lips as he heard the tinkle of the glasses gave the game away. Vladimir picked up his glass, sat back and allowed his cousin to relate the tale in whatever way he saw fit. Both Tim and Halim, who knew little of the detail, listened in silence as Momchil, in slow deliberate tones, began the story.

*

When his phone rang Hristo was just finishing his coffee. At first he assumed it would be his wife, but as soon as he saw an unfamiliar number being displayed he knew it was the museum calling him. The curator was straight to the point. The Director from the museum in Sofia had arrived and was asking to see him. Hristo called the young waiter over and paid for his meal. Although he was now in something of a hurry he did not forget his manners and thanked the young man for an excellent lunch. Purposefully he got up from his seat and left the restaurant. The layout of the city of Veliko Tarnovo is such that nearly all places can be reached most easily on foot so within ten minutes Hristo was back at the museum.

"Hristo Genkov, Mayor of Arbanasi," he said offering his hand.

The Director shook his hand warmly and formally introduced himself and all his associates.

"The curator of this delightful museum and his assistant, Petya, you have already met, I believe?" Hristo affirmed this with a smile in their direction.

The Director of the National Historical Museum in Sofia was more excited than he might have appeared. His had been a long stint as Director and although he had been a very effective and competent steward of the museum, up until now nothing very remarkable had happened. Although he had sat politely while the young woman Petya had given him an earnest and detailed account of how she had aged the artefact, it was in truth unnecessary. He had known at once what he was looking at. The Director would have been stirred by the discovery of any artefact of this age and in such perfect condition, but his interest in this particular object went way beyond that. Like the mayor he was completely familiar with the legend of the icon of Arbanasi and he believed in it. He knew that he was looking at the piece itself.

"Tell me, Mr Genkov, the young man who found the icon; has he told you anything about the circumstances of the find?" the Director asked.

"Yes, he certainly has. The circumstances were quite remarkable," replied Hristo.

The Director became very animated. "Tell me, tell me all about it."

Hristo then recounted the tale exactly as it had been told to him. He could see that, unlike the curator who was very sceptical, this time he had a very receptive audience. When Hristo had concluded the story the Director looked at him intently.

"Do you believe him, Mr Genkov?" he asked simply.

Hristo thought for a moment. He wanted his words to have the maximum impact.

"I am sure that every detail of the story is true," he replied.

"It is as I expected," the Director said with authority. He then turned to address the whole group.

"This confirms the remarkable legend of the miraculous icon of the Virgin Mary. It is the very same icon that was buried by nuns from Arbanasi fleeing the Turkish invaders more than six hundred years ago. According to the legend it was found at a later stage of Ottoman rule by a shepherd boy. Since then its whereabouts have not been known. I have studied this subject for more than twenty years and have come to the view that it was buried again by the shepherd boy around the time of the second Tarnovo uprising. It now appears likely that he buried the icon in the very place where he had originally found it. Why, I cannot say. I suspect it had something to do with the uprising which is purported to have started in Arbanasi. This is a remarkable moment."

Petya listened with interest and admiration to the Director. As far as she was concerned he was a most remarkable man. Although a lifelong historian dealing in scientifically verifiable facts he took on the wholly inexplicable detail of the legend with utter ease. He simply believed. To Petya this was what elevated him to a higher plain than his contemporaries. The first thing is to accept the facts, however unlikely and then eventually the explanation will follow. This approach is what she had always believed in and strived for. This is what she had been trying to get across to Halim.

Chapter Eleven

That evening, more than ever before, Petya was desperate to see Halim. She had so much to tell him. Above all she believed that the icon could somehow be the key to explaining his strange encounters. She must see him. Halim was already deep in thought about the icon and all that surrounded its discovery having been told all about it by Momchil. This was yet another link to the past that fitted with his vision of the old house. Somehow he must find the connection. He knew that he needed help with this and was on the verge of calling Petya when the phone rang.

"Hi, Petya. I was just about to phone you. You have beaten me to it."

Petya was brimming over with news and excitement. "I must see you. I am so sorry we could not speak earlier at the museum. I have so much to tell you. Can you come over now?"

Halim was a little taken aback by her insistent, even desperate tone.

"Is everything alright?" Halim asked somewhat anxiously.

"Yes, of course. More than alright, in fact. When can you be here? I could meet you at the hotel on Gurko Street, where we had coffee and cake. It's your turn to pay by the way."

Halim was momentarily stung by the reminder of his impolite behaviour on the day they met, but soon realised it was intended as a light hearted remark.

"Yes, I will pay, but tonight? It could be difficult."

Petya was having none of this. She intended to see Halim tonight, difficult or not.

"Get a taxi. I will pay."

Halim could see that Petya was not going to take no for an answer.

"I will ask Margot or Tim if they are going anywhere near Veliko Tarnovo tonight. I will ring you back."

Halim had wanted to speak to Petya, but was rocked back on his heels by her insistence that they meet up right away. He wanted to see her because he liked her and he valued her ability to think outside the box and he needed help to make sense of all that was happening. Nevertheless, he was not altogether naïve and was becoming more than aware that her desire to see him was based on something else entirely. She was continuing to make him feel uncomfortable. Still he was committed now so he went down to the living room in the hope of finding Tim or Margot. He found Margot sitting at the table reading. She looked up with a smile.

"Hi Halim, are you OK."

"Yes, I am fine, thank you. Margot, are either of you planning to go to Veliko Tarnovo tonight?"

Margot looked a little surprised. She could tell that Halim was on edge.

"No, but if you need a lift I don't mind taking you."

Halim was about to thank her, but decline the offer when Tim came in from the kitchen.

"A pressing engagement with Petya, I assume?" Tim said in a teasing tone that was lost on Halim, but not on Margot.

She at once intervened on Halim's behalf. "If Halim wants to go to VT it is none of your business what he wishes to do there," she told her husband firmly.

Tim took the admonishment in his stride. "Actually, Vladimir said earlier that he was taking Momchil for a drink in town tonight. He will give you a lift, I am sure. Pop over and ask him."

"You ask him, Tim," said Margot. "Halim hardly knows him."

Tim thought the matter through quickly. Suddenly he decided that he wouldn't mind going for a drink himself, especially if someone else was driving.

"Come on, Halim. We'll go and see him now," he said and turning headed for the door. Halim followed.

Next door the three cousins were all sitting in the garden enjoying the early evening sunshine. An hour earlier Rada had finally been persuaded by Nedyalko to leave, although her misgivings about her daughter were far from allayed. Vladimir was seated facing the gate and so saw his visitors at once. As he rose to greet them, Momchil stood too and turned towards the gate.

The girl had her back to them, but remaining in her seat she looked around with a smile of welcome on her face. Halim was transfixed. Her beauty defied description. Now seeing her close up for the first time he could see that her face was lovely beyond compare. Strangely though he felt it was a familiar face that he was seeing anew. Suddenly, inexplicably he saw himself riding a chestnut horse. It was a vision that made no sense, he could not even ride, but it was so strong. All at once he realised that he was riding to meet her, this girl. He had loved her. All at once his inward eye was bombarded with visions; the house; him standing by the oak tree; he saw another girl. She was her sister. Halim continued to stare at Denitsa and unerringly she met his gaze. In his mind's eye he dismounted from the chestnut steed landing only a foot from her. He could feel her warm breath on his face. Halim was losing control. He put his head in his hands, closing his eyes. He fought to focus on the here and now, here in this garden with Denitsa. Was that even her name? He remembered. She had been annoyed with him. His horse had startled her. But later she had smiled.

"Rayna, my name is Rayna," she had said.

When she spoke, a simple, shy word of greeting, the last of his composure deserted him completely.

"Zdraveĭte!" said Denitsa, one of the few words of Bulgarian that Halim understood and could repeat, but he remained tongue tied, staring.

"Zdraveĭte!" replied Tim, trying to save Halim's embarrassment, but neither Denitsa nor Halim heard him.

Denitsa had noticed Halim's apparent paralysis and she too felt fixed in this moment, unable and unwilling to move. She too was captivated. She knew this handsome face, this softness of manner, but how? Who was he?

"Hello! Can we join in this staring game?" interjected Tim, cut loose from Margot's control.

His crassness broke the spell and the two young people tried to regain their dignity, but both found it hard to avert their eyes from each other.

Tim continued to try and restore normality. "Are you still going to VT for a drink?" he enquired of Vladimir.

"Yes," replied Vladimir, still dazed by what he had witnessed. "Why, do you and Halim want to come?"

"I thought I might," said Tim "but Halim here wanted a lift into town to see Petya. Mind you, I am not sure if he still wants to go."

"I do not want to, but I must." said Halim, unaware of the inference in Tim's words.

Denitsa felt an irrational rush of jealousy. "Who is Petya?"

The words were out before she realised what she had said.

"Just some ugly girl he knows," said Tim, but Denitsa was equally out of tune with Tim's sense of humour.

"So she is not your girlfriend, Halim?"

"No, absolutely not," replied Halim rather too emphatically.

"I am glad," she said shocked at her own boldness.

Momchil equally was not sure what to make of his sister's behaviour and decided to bring proceedings to an end.

"I am thirsty," he announced. "Are we going now?"

Both Tim and Vladimir gave a little laugh and stood up to leave.

"Are you coming, Deni?" Vladimir asked finally, still worrying about his young cousin.

"No, go ahead. I promised Mama I would go to bed early and if I don't she will be bound to find out." And with a gentle smile playing on her beautiful lips she went into the house.

*

Petya arrived at the Gurko Hotel twenty minutes ahead of the time they had agreed. She sat upright in the chair biting her nails, a habit she thought she had conquered. For years her various boyfriends had been desperate to spend time with her whilst she had always retained a measure of cool detachment. She did not like this sudden reversal, but seemed powerless to do anything about it. She was aware that she had been unreasonably insistent about seeing Halim that night, but she could not help herself. When he finally arrived she shot out of her seat like a coiled spring causing Halim to take an instinctive, but involuntary step backwards. It felt more like the launching of an attack than a greeting.

"I'm sorry, I nearly knocked you over. I'm just so pleased to see you."

As she spoke she realised she was making matters worse. Halim looked quite anxious. Petya struggled, not entirely successfully, to get on top of her emotions.

She sat down and tried to make some small talk while a renegade voice within her shouted, "Tell him you love him. Kiss him!" but she just about managed to keep the renegade under control.

"How are Margot and Tim? They are such lovely people," she began.

"They are fine. They send their regards," he replied rather nervously.

Halim was spooked by the sudden swings in mood. He wasn't sure what was coming next. He was right to worry.

"I have so much to tell you." she said with a sudden renewed intensity. "Can you stay all night?"

Halim started to regret that he had come. She sensed it and realised it was her doing. If she was not careful he would get up and run out again.

"Get a grip of yourself, Petya," she said to herself.

She resolved to say nothing more until she had calmed herself and slowly she did start to get a grip. When she seemed calmer Halim ventured a reply.

"Unfortunately I only have a couple of hours. My neighbour is giving me a lift home at ten."

Somehow she rode the disappointment. "Is that your neighbour, Vladimir, the finder of the icon?"

"Yes, he is very kind. So what did you make of the icon?" he asked.

She felt herself relax. They had found safer ground.

With her anxiety level for the moment reduced Petya decided to tell Halim her big news from the museum, but as she started to do so her jealousy came to the fore again as she recalled seeing Halim talking and smiling with Desi.

"I saw Desi talking to you. What were you talking about?"

Halim thought this an odd question and was surprised by the tone in Petya's voice, but made no comment on it. Instead he simply answered the question.

"She told me that the important visitor who arrived at the museum just after me was the Director of the National Historical Museum in Sofia," Halim replied.

Petya looked at him as if she barely believed him, then after a pause she resumed.

"Yes, he is an amazing man," she continued "There is nothing he does not know about Bulgaria during Ottoman rule. He believes your neighbour has discovered the icon that is central to a local legend. According to that legend the icon, originally buried by nuns in the fourteenth century, was found towards the end of the seventeenth century and then reburied soon after. He believes the events are connected to the second Tarnovo uprising."

"What did you say?" exclaimed Halim suddenly.

For a moment Petya lost the thread of her story and just stared at Halim.

"The second Tarnovo uprising," he continued, "I have always had a deep curiosity for this event. I never understood why. It is connected:

the icon, the vision of the old house, my feeling that I have been here before and even the girl. It is *all* connected."

Petya was suddenly alarmed. "What girl?" she demanded.

Halim was dragged away from his thoughts back into the here and now.

"Vladimir's cousin, Denitsa. I met her tonight, but it's as if I know her."

Petya's face became anxious and twisted. "Why would you think you know her if you have just met? Did she come on to you?"

Halim was completely taken aback by this sudden and unexpected line of questioning. His first reaction was to defend Denitsa's honour.

"Of course not. She hardly knows me."

"Why would that stop her?" replied Petya bitterly.

"Look, you do not even know the girl. Why are you acting this way?"

Still Petya pressed him for more information and he found himself playing down his assertion that he and Denitsa had possibly met before. He did not want to talk about her in this way.

"Maybe she just looks like someone I know. I am sure it is not important," he maintained although as he said it he became increasingly sure that it was important.

His own thoughts were completely consumed by Denitsa and Petya's words had shocked and upset him. He could see that Petya's feelings for him were again threatening to get out of hand. He had to get away. He was about to give some excuse and leave when Petya dropped the subject of Denitsa and resumed her news from the museum.

"There is going to be a big exhibition based on the second Tarnovo uprising. I am to take charge of it and it will be opened by the Director from the museum in Sofia. There will be exhibits collected from a number of museums in Sofia and throughout Bulgaria and brought here. I am so excited about it."

Halim too found the prospect of such an exhibition very exciting. "You must be very proud. It is a great opportunity for you," he said, glad to be back on safe ground.

Petya continued. "Apparently the National Historical Museum in Sofia has a sword believed to have been used during the Tarnovo uprising to slay one of the leaders of the Turkish forces. It is going to be featured in the exhibition."

All of a sudden she worried that as a Turk Halim would be uncomfortable discussing a period of such disharmony between their two countries. Had she upset him again? She expressed this concern to him.

"It is a matter of historical fact," was his reply. "It is also well documented that the Ottoman Empire was based on ruthless oppression. I condemn this as you would."

*

Denitsa was feeling something more wonderful than she thought possible. She hadn't eaten, but forgot she was hungry. She had hardly slept the night before, but forgot she was tired. Her eyes were sore, but she felt no pain. It was absurd, but her feelings about Halim made all other feeling impossible. There was simply no space for them, no point to them. She sat motionless on the bed and just allowed this feeling to wash over her. Her body felt weightless. A smile crept across her face. In her mind's eye she saw herself with Halim, but suddenly she wasn't sure whether she was seeing her future or her past. She had planned to ring her mother, but what could she possibly say to her?

*

The three friends, Momchil, Vladimir and Tim, were seated outside at the Humphrey Bogart bar just off the square. In the square itself a group of women dressed in the Bulgarian national costume were dancing to traditional music played by a small folk group. The women looked resplendent in their red skirts and white blouses, embroidered with black and red and brightly decorated with coins, beads and silk.

"I love the dancing," said Tim "but I must admit the music drives me crazy. It is so repetitive."

"I am glad you like the dancing," replied Momchil. "I don't like the music either and of course I am unable to appreciate the dancing. Denitsa tried to make me learn some dances a few years ago, but it was hopeless. She said it was nothing to do with my being blind, I just had no rhythm."

"That sounds a bit unfair," said Vladimir. "I would think not being able to see could be a slight disadvantage," he added with unintended irony. "Still, you can't complain. The wonderful thing about your sister is she believes you capable of almost anything and more often than not she is shown to be correct. So if she says you have no rhythm she is probably right."

"Don't worry, cousin, I would never complain about her," Momchil replied.

"So she doesn't only look like an angel, she is one," observed Tim. The two cousins smiled and nodded their agreement.

Soon the conversation moved on to the subject on everyone's mind: the discovery of the icon and what it all meant. Tim was firmly in the same camp as Uncle Nedyalko and was eager to know what Vladimir would make from the find. Momchil, took the same line as his mother had with Nedyalko, only Tim was more persistent.

"The icon may be a precious religious artefact, but it is also valuable. You found it, Vlado, so you must have some claim to it."

"Maybe I have," replied Vladimir "but at the moment I am more worried about getting to the bottom of all these mysteries around Denitsa and also concerning Galena. The strange circumstances in which I found the icon make me inclined to believe that all these things are connected."

Tim remained sceptical and only half believed Vladimir's story about the mournful voice that had supposedly drawn him to where the icon was buried. Vladimir liked and respected Tim, but he could see that the conversation was going nowhere and that Momchil was getting agitated listening to Tim.

"Let's have another beer," he suggested.

Travelling back in the car Halim was very quiet. He had so much on his mind he could barely think straight. Petya's mood swings and intensity had really unsettled him and he was clearly in danger of being dragged into a relationship that he did not want. She even frightened him at times. The only thing he knew for certain was that he needed to see and speak to Denitsa. He was dazzled by her and desperately wanted to spend some time with her, talking to her and getting to know her better. Also he believed that Denitsa could be the key to understanding everything that had happened since his arrival.

*

Petya walked home through the old town, along the River Yantra and across the bridge passing the Boris Denev State Art Gallery and the impressive Assens' monument from where she had an exceptional view of the old houses stacked one on top of the other on the opposite hill. Tonight however she did not give any thought to the beauty of the town where she had grown up of which she was normally so proud. Petya was filled with an irrational jealousy towards someone that she had never met. She regretted Halim's reluctance to stay the night. She was an experienced lover and there was no doubt in her mind that she was capable of making Halim a slave to her charms, but at the moment she saw clearly that he was in thrall to some stupid peasant girl. Having been denied the opportunity to work her magic on Halim she decided to pay a visit to the little trollop the very next morning. No country harlot was going to stand between her and the man she wanted.

The next morning Petya stood at the coach station waiting impatiently for the bus to Arbanasi. She had not given any proper thought about what she would say to the little slut known as Denitsa, but she intended to frighten her and make it clear she was to go nowhere near Halim. As she stood there with the jealousy burning inside her a sign written van passed her bearing the logo, 'Vladimir – Man with a Van'. Immediately she remembered Halim telling her about his neighbour's business and that he employed Denitsa and her brother. It had amused Halim that the logo was in English. This was them. The van turned right at the end of the road and as she scurried after it the van stopped outside a store selling washing machines and fridges. As Petya approached the driver got out and walked towards the entrance to the store. On the pavement side a young woman was helping another man out of the van.

Petya stopped about ten metres from where the girl stood. She looked at her with hate in her eyes, but the girl, realising she was looking at her, addressed Petya with politeness.

"Hello, can we help you at all?" she asked.

Petya moved closer and for the first time Denitsa felt alarm. She thought the woman who she had never seen before was going to strike her. She was arm in arm with her brother and so he felt Denitsa's anxiety too, only more strongly. Believing his sister was under some sort of threat Momchil took a step forward.

"Who are you? What do you want from us?" he demanded.

As he stepped towards her Petya realised for the first time that the man was blind. With typical correctness Halim had never told her that.

"Well?" said Momchil forcefully.

At that moment Petya's courage failed her and she became flustered and unsure. With a final cold stare at Denitsa she turned on her heal and hurried away.

Momchil heard her go and relaxed a little although he still kept a tight hold on his sister's arm.

"Who the hell was that?" he asked.

"I have no idea, Momchil. I have never seen the woman before in my life," Denitsa replied.

"A woman!" Momchil exclaimed in surprise. "I assumed it was a man."

Denitsa stroked his arm with her free hand. "No, it was a woman, but no less frightening for that."

It was true that she did not know who the woman was, but oddly she had an idea who it could be.

Chapter Twelve

Margot was standing in the kitchen writing a shopping list. The thought of going to the supermarket always put her in a bad mood. She had just come in from the garden having gone out to ask Tim if he wanted anything. She didn't know why she bothered as he always gave the same answer:

"A crate of beer, please; Zagorka if they have it."

"So you don't want any eggs or bread or cheese or vegetables or floor cleaner?" Margot had enquired, but the sarcasm was wasted on Tim.

"No, you're right, some of that asparagus we had last week would be nice," he had replied, unwittingly making his wife's mood considerably worse.

So when Halim rushed into the kitchen to say that Tim had put his foot down a hole and seemed to be in a lot of pain she was not at her most sympathetic.

"And what exactly does he expect me to do?" she asked much to Halim's astonishment.

He stood looking at Margot expecting her to say something else, but he was met by stony silence. He tried again.

"I am not sure whether he can stand up," he added.

Margot was not really interested, but she realised that it was inappropriate to leave the problem to Halim.

"I am sorry, Halim. I am coming now. A kick up the backside should do the trick."

Halim was baffled. "Won't that make Tim hurt more?" he asked with genuine concern.

"I hope so," said Margot and headed outside to see the invalid with Halim trailing anxiously behind her.

"I will never understand the English ways," he said to himself.

"For crying out loud, Margot, where have you been? I'm in agony here."

Margot could see that Tim was indeed in some pain and her mood of indifference melted just enough to think practically.

"I'm going shopping now. I'll drop you off at the hospital in VT. Maybe they should have a look at it. I'm sure it's nothing, though."

Tim wasn't so sure. His ankle hurt like hell and, although he had never broken a bone before, he imagined this is how it would feel. With Halim's help he got to his feet and hobbled inside to find a fresh shirt and a clean pair of jeans. When he finally emerged Margot's attitude had not softened greatly.

"Christ, Tim! You're going to the hospital, not to a party."

"I can't go looking like some reprobate," he replied climbing slowly and with real difficulty into the front passenger seat. Margot gave some last minute instructions to Halim and drove away towards town.

By the time they arrived at the hospital Margot was starting to feel guilty about how she had been with Tim. Although it was true that Margot did almost all of the shopping, which she hated, and most household chores she did not really have a case against Tim as he did all the house maintenance and improvements as well as the gardening. This had been the division of labour between them ever since arriving in Bulgaria and although it was organised along traditional gender lines it was not inherently unfair.

"Tim, I'm sorry I was a cow before and I am sorry about your ankle. Is it any better?"

"I can't tell until I try to stand on it," he replied. "I've probably just sprained it. I can't quite work out how I did it. I think I put my foot on an uneven piece of ground and the next thing I was in agony."

Margot pulled the car up as close to the entrance of the hospital as possible. She got out and helped Tim into reception where he collapsed into a chair.

"I'll stay with you. I can do the shopping another time," Margot suggested, but Tim declined the offer.

"There's no point you hanging around, I'll probably be waiting for hours. I've got my phone. I'll ring you when they've finished with me."

Margot could see the sense in what Tim was saying and promised to return as soon as he rang. She gave him an affectionate peck on the cheek and left. Now on his own Tim looked around for the first time and realised he was the only person in the waiting area. His first inclination was to wonder whether he was in the right place, however his Bulgarian was good enough to decipher the various signs which told him he was indeed in the Bulgarian equivalent of Accident and Emergency.

Within five minutes Tim was sitting on a bed with an A & E doctor examining his foot. He squeezed Tim's ankle and he let out a cry of pain. The doctor did away with the formality of asking Tim if it hurt when he did that.

"I think it is broken," he said.

A porter with a wheelchair was summoned and Tim was wheeled off to see an orthopaedic surgeon who seemed to be ready for him when he arrived. Without bothering to get Tim out of the wheelchair he repeated the same method of diagnosis used by his colleague. Tim yelped obligingly and was shunted off for an X-ray. Less than ten minutes later he was back in front of the surgeon with the X-ray on his lap. The surgeon looked briefly at the photograph, took a pair of scissors and sliced the leg of Tim's brand new jeans right up to the crutch.

"They cost 70 leva!" Tim exclaimed helplessly.

The doctor hesitated briefly and looked at Tim quizzically under the misconception that he had said something relevant to the injury.

"It doesn't matter," said Tim resignedly.

Ten minutes later he was dumped back in the waiting room, his leg plastered up to the knee. Tim was given neither crutches nor sticks, nor any information on how to obtain them.

"What do I do now?" he asked the porter.

"Go home!" he was told and the porter headed off up the corridor pushing the wheelchair towards his next victim.

Tim sat there trying to work out what to do. Although troubled by the aftercare, he had never been attended to by a team of medics so quickly and efficiently. He looked at his watch. It was less than half an hour since Margot had left him there. He could not help but be impressed. Tim located his phone somewhere within the wreckage of his trousers and called Margot. To Tim's surprise the phone was answered by Halim.

"Can I speak to Margot?" he said without bothering to ask for an explanation.

"She is shopping," he was told "And Tim is at the hospital."

"I know that!"

Tim was shouting now and slowly it dawned on Halim that it was Tim on the phone.

"I am sorry, Tim. Margot left her phone on the kitchen table and I thought it best to answer it."

"You did well." said Tim reassuringly, whilst cursing Margot under his breath for again forgetting her phone.

Tim told Halim the full story of his encounter with Bulgarian A & E and explained that he was now marooned with no means of contacting Margot. Halim made the very sensible suggestion that Tim should contact Vladimir.

"If you remember, they only had two or three small jobs in Veliko Tarnovo. They should be finishing about now," said Halim, "And if you are lucky they might still be in town."

Tim thanked him for his common sense and immediately followed up with a call to Vladimir.

"It is not a problem. We are just finishing. We can be there in half an hour," said Vladimir in response to Tim's cry for help and soon afterwards the old transit proclaiming 'Man with a Van' pulled into the hospital car park. Tim was unceremoniously hauled into the van as if he were just another payload and soon the three musketeers, as Denitsa continued to call them, were on their way back to Arbanasi with their human cargo. When they arrived Vladimir and Momchil half carried Tim into the house under the careful direction of Denitsa. So concentrated was she on the performance of her task she did not at first realise that Halim was standing in the hallway to receive them.

When she did at last notice him she found Halim staring at her, almost examining her. In return she fixed her beautiful brown eyes on him and for a moment they both forgot about Tim's plight. When Tim broke the silence it was as if he was speaking to them from another place.

"Any word from Margot?" he asked.

Somehow Halim managed to drag his eyes away from Denitsa, but still found it impossible to react to what Tim was asking him. Instead he simply repeated his earlier bulletin.

"She has gone shopping," he said dreamily.

Tim looked up at Halim and at once realised he was unlikely to get much sense out of him.

Then suddenly out of nowhere it happened, the moment of recognition. Denitsa's blood ran cold as her eyes widened in disbelief. Her mouth opened but no sound came out. The vision, the battle scene, the young man lying dead with her standing over him. It was him; it was Halim. All the colour drained from her face as she ran from the room knocking over a chair and a small table as she went. She stumbled onto her knees hurting herself, but was at once back on her feet and running faster than before towards the front door. Momchil felt his sister's terror and stood to try and follow her, but Halim held him back.

"I will go," he said firmly.

Momchil cursed his own disabilities. He was tired of having to leave important things to someone else.

"Then go, go quickly," he demanded and Halim ran in pursuit of the fleeing girl.

When he caught up with her Denitsa was lying face down in Vladimir's hallway, her loud sobs partially muted by the woven carpet. She did not look round, but knew who stood there.

"Go away! Leave me alone. I am dangerous to you. Go!"

To her great relief he ignored her request. Halim remained and she, against her better judgement, was glad of it. Slowly her sobs subsided as he quietly knelt down beside her. He laid his hand on her bare shoulder and gently raised her. No longer in charge of her own actions Denitsa turned her face towards him and he lowered his head to meet her lips with his.

*

Galena had been in a state of turmoil throughout the whole weekend. She had been mulling over all that Denitsa had said, particularly her assertion that Galena and the vegetable plot belonging to Galena's family were familiar to her. Thinking about it now she remembered that her conviction that she had a sister was often strongest when she was working the field alone. Somehow she had memory of two sisters working there together. Impossible as it seemed there was only one explanation: Denitsa was her sister.

Galena had also spent a lot of time thinking about Vladimir. After so many barren years hoping that he would notice her, she had virtually given up and now, all of a sudden, he seemed to have woken up to her existence. As the weekend progressed and he did not contact her she started to wonder whether she had after all imagined his interest in her. Then on Sunday evening he had rung her bursting with news and she was sure that more than anyone he had wanted to tell her about the icon. The mayor, Hristo Genkov, had asked the family not to talk about the icon until its authenticity had been verified, but Vladimir had told her nevertheless. He described to her the circumstances of his discovery which was the reason the mayor knew it was the icon of the legend. Best of all, amongst all the things Vladimir had said to her on Sunday evening he had not forgotten to tell her she was beautiful.

Galena had spent Monday working in the field and was there again the following day when Vladimir called her. They had been planning to meet up that afternoon, but Vladimir explained that his neighbour had broken his ankle and needed his help to get home from the hospital. It did not look as if they would be able to see each other after all. Galena had only met Tim a few times and found him charming. British men had such lovely manners towards women, she thought to herself.

"Tell him I hope he recovers soon," she said "We can meet up another day."

Galena was not put out by the turn of events. She did not feel any desperation about not seeing Vladimir. She could summon him up in her thoughts as she had often done before, but from now on the images that would flash before her would not be tinged with sadness. Anyway, she was happy working in the field and would never again feel alone here. Galena smiled to herself. She felt content. For as long as she could remember she had a notion that a part of her was missing, but now for the first time she felt whole. She did have a sister and the man she had loved for so long was learning to love her too.

*

When the sword arrived from the museum in Sofia the administrator called Petya to the office to sign for it.

"I do not want to take responsibility for something so valuable," the administrator had explained, but Petya was only too glad to receive it.

This meant she could spend some time examining it before handing it over to the museum's curator to be formally listed. Alone in one of the many unused offices she took it carefully from its elaborate packaging. Petya saw at once that this was in fact a Turkish sword known as a Yataghan. The hilt was made of bone, or possibly ivory, and the pommel was flared. It had a short, slightly curved blade, sharp on only one edge with a fine point. Petya was confused. She had been told that this sword was used by a Bulgarian to slay one of the leaders of the Turkish forces. Just to be sure Petya searched on her phone for an image of a Yataghan. The image she found was virtually identical to the sword lying on the desk in front of her. She sat trying to recall what she knew of the second uprising. For a moment she considered ringing the museum Director from Sofia. She was on the verge of doing so when the explanation suddenly dawned on her.

As far as she recalled the uprising started when the rebel army attacked and overwhelmed a small garrison in the surrounding neighbourhood. Many historians believed it was the garrison at Arbanasi that had been hit first. She realised that given the superiority of Ottoman weapons the rebels probably abandoned their own swords and daggers in favour of those of the Turkish soldiers. It therefore made sense that in subsequent battles some Ottoman soldiers had been slain by their own weapons. Petya reached a further conclusion. If it was true that the uprising had started there then it followed that the person who had wielded this sword against their Turkish foe had been a warrior from Arbanasi.

Again she thought about Halim. In fact she never stopped thinking about him, but here at last she had something that would really interest him and get his attention on her. He was incredibly interested in the second uprising and certainly the stupid little peasant girl that he was so interested in would have nothing to say on the subject. Petya touched the fine point of the blade with her thumb. Momentarily she imagined plunging it through the pretty little slut's neck. It was indeed a fine weapon. She picked up her phone again and called Halim. It rang for quite a long time and then went to messages. She dialled again with the same outcome. Why did he not answer? Where was he and who was he with? She knew that if she left a message she might have to wait an eternity for him to reply. Petya was not prepared to wait.

She made a rash decision. As far as she knew the curator was not yet aware that the sword had arrived and, given that the museum administrator usually went the whole day without speaking to anyone, she could be reasonably sure he would not find out. She would take a chance. She carefully returned the sword to its original packaging, grabbed her bag and cardigan and hurriedly left the building. As she bustled along towards the centre of town she was trying to work out the best way of getting to Arbanasi. Given the immense value of her package taking a bus seemed too much of a risk and given the urgency to find Halim it would also be too slow. As she passed the Gurko hotel she saw a taxi parked outside with the driver leaning against the side of the car smoking a cigarette. Her mind was made up for her.

When the cabby asked Petya where she wanted to go she realised for the first time that she still had no idea where in Arbanasi Halim lived. The taxi headed off in the direction of the village with the driver eyeing her with suspicion in his mirror. He could see that she was very agitated and was starting to wonder what was in the large package.

"Have you ever given a lift to an English couple who live in Arbanasi?" she asked suddenly. "Their names are Tim and Margot."

The driver thought for a while. "I don't recall it," he replied, "But one of my colleagues speaks English and usually takes the English fares. I will ring him."

Two minutes later the taxi driver was off the phone. His colleague knew an Englishman in Arbanasi called Tim and had given him directions to the house. Fifteen minutes later he pulled up outside Tim's and Margot's house, still wondering what the connection was between a pretty young Bulgarian girl, a middle aged British couple and a large package. However, he decided not to enquire, took his fare and drove away.

Petya stood on the road unsure how to proceed. All at once the rashness of her actions came home to her. If her absence from the museum was noticed she would be in big trouble. If it was further discovered that she had the ancient and priceless sword with her she would not only lose her job, she would probably never work in a museum again. Why had she brought the sword? Suddenly nothing was clear. Halim had not answered his phone and it was perfectly possible that he was not even in Arbanasi and the whole hare brained scheme would have been for nothing. Petya was looking for reassurance and was gratified to see that Tim's car, the one she had recently been taken home in, was parked in the drive. At least she was at the right house. Petya looked about her to get a feel for the neighbourhood before approaching the house. As she did so she suddenly saw Halim about one hundred metres away in the street. A surge of excitement came over her and she started to walk and then to run in that direction. As she drew closer she began to call his name. Halim looked up and took a short step in the direction of her voice. A split second later he turned to speak to someone nearby and Petya suddenly realised that he was not alone. A young woman in jeans and tee shirt stood alongside him. Petya recognised her instantly. An overwhelming jealousy took hold of her and as she got closer she could plainly see from the looks exchanged between them that this was a young couple infatuated with each other. She was furious.

"What do you want with her?" she demanded.

Unable to control her feelings she continued, becoming ever more offensive with her questions.

"Your little whore Denitsa, what do you want with the little bitch?"

Both Denitsa and Halim were shocked by the bitterness in her voice. As she had suspected at the time this was the woman who recently confronted her on the street in Veliko Tarnovo. Denitsa knew nothing about this woman who seemed to think she had a claim on Halim. The woman looked at her with loathing. Denitsa instinctively put her arm around Halim's waist as if for protection which enraged Petya yet more.

Before she had time to think Petya drew the sword from the packaging without knowing what she intended to do with it. Denitsa looked on in horror. Halim moved towards her imploring her to calm down.

"I brought this for you. It is the ancient sword I spoke about. I thought it would interest you. I have risked everything and here you are with the peasant girl," she said, brandishing the sword, gripping it so tight her knuckles whitened.

Petya set her gaze on Denitsa who felt terrified. She could see quite clearly what the woman intended to do with the sword. Halim also feared the worst and made a sudden grab for the sword. He and Petya tumbled over. All at once Denitsa saw again the vision that she had seen on her first morning in Arbanasi. She saw Bayram dying, she knew his name, but this time she could see that it was not her that had killed him, but her friend Vladislav. He had died in battle and a girl that was surely her was leaning over his body. This girl had loved him.

Petya got slowly to her feet, but Halim remained motionless on the floor, the sword impaled in his chest.

Chapter Thirteen

As they had done on each Sunday since his death Vladimir, Galena and Denitsa gathered for a silent prayer at the exact spot where Halim had died. The two sisters stood hand in hand. No one spoke. Today, however, they had a further assignment. Vladimir carried a spade and had a rucksack on his back within which he carried the precious icon of the Virgin Mary, inside its silver cover and wrapped in cloth. In trying to persuade the museum to release the icon Vladimir had been completely honest as to his intentions. The mayor of Arbanasi, Hristo Genkov had proved to be a great ally in the affair. It was he who had contacted the Director of the National Historical Museum in Sofia and asked him to intervene. Both the mayor and the museum director understood what Vladimir intended and approved of his plan.

The solemn trio took the lane out of the village towards the forest. They then followed the forest path until the point where Vladimir only a few months earlier had diverted from the path in answer to the cries that he had at first believed to be the sound of goats and later recognised as a human cry. As they approached the point where the icon had been discovered the mournful voice could again be heard. The three friends were unmoved. The two girls looked on as Vladimir went about his business carefully and methodically. When he felt that the hole he had dug was sufficiently deep to both preserve and conceal the icon he took the ancient artefact from his rucksack. Without either emotion or ceremony he placed the icon in the hole and covered it with earth. As soon as the icon was buried the voice ceased. Vladimir turned and hugged his cousin tightly aware that her loss was of a different magnitude to his own. Quietly they left that place with no intention of ever returning.

Part Three

Turkey
2307 AD

Chapter Fourteen

Yuliana was sitting waiting for the monorail to Istanbul with her best friend Rositsa. Rosi, as everyone liked to call her, was a pretty girl with plenty to say for herself. Yuliana on the other hand was quieter, but had a serenity about her that made conversation seem superfluous. She was so extremely beautiful that people who met her had an inclination just to look rather than to speak. Yuliana and Rosi had arrived in Turkey the day before and they were excited and looking forward to their trip. Both of the girls were eighteen and between high school and university. Istanbul was the first stop on a gap year odyssey that would take them half way around the world.

Whereas Yuliana was looking forward to finding out about modern Istanbul that had recently become the administrative capital of the EU's eastern zone, Rosi was consumed with more down to earth matters. She had been going on about how handsome the Turkish boys were ever since they passed through the border from Bulgaria so, as a young man sat down opposite them, Yuliana was not surprised to get a strong nudge in the ribs from her friend. Yuliana looked up and found herself staring straight into the young Turk's eyes. All at once she felt weak and was certain she was going to faint. The young man continued to meet her gaze.

"I am sorry to stare," he said, but gave no proper excuse for continuing to do so.

The girl was so ravishing and had such magnetic beauty that once his eyes had fallen upon her it became an extreme act of will to draw his glance away and for quite some time he lacked both the will and inclination to do so. As they looked at each other they both saw in their mind's eye a vision of the two of them together, but they were both unsure whether they were seeing their future or their past.

Footnote:

If you have enjoyed 'The Icon of Arbanasi' I would be grateful if you could leave a review on Amazon.

Go to https://www.amazon.co.uk/Icon-Arbanasi-Geoff-Hart-ebook/dp/B011A7RP5M, click on 'customer reviews' and then click on 'write a customer review'.

You might also enjoy my other books, Bulgaria: Unfinished Business and Second Time Lucky, also available on Amazon.

Many thanks,
Geoff Hart, author

Printed in Great Britain
by Amazon

26414459R00086